SECOND SIGHT
FOR SORE EYES

Books by Paul Carroll

The Black Pages
A Death in the Family
The Undying and the Dead
Second Sight of Sort Eyes

The Rebirth Cycle
Balor Reborn
The Hounds of Hell
The Blood of Leap
Old Gods & Wicked Things

Standalone Titles
Tales of the Fantastical (Vol. 1)
Stepping Forward

Anthologies
Dublin's Fierce City
Fierce Mighty
Fierce New World
Fierce & Proud
Fiercepunk

paulcarrollwriter.com

The Black Pages

The Magic Man Book 1

Second Sight for Sore Eyes

Paul Carroll

First published by Paul Carroll at paulcarrollwriter.com

Copyright © Paul Carroll 2018, 2020

ISBN: 9798694551038

For Gareth, Gary, Helen and Kat,
for making me a happier person.

Table of Contents

℘ROLOGUE

Dublin City at night can be quiet, depending on the night and the weather. Some parts of the city sink into a calm silence after sunset, a peace that lasts for a few hours before the pubs eject their patrons into the streets. Before then, one could be forgiven for thinking it a quiet city. You could stand by the Liffey and pretend it wasn't filled with filth, listening instead to the water lapping against the stone banks while the occasional car or bus passed.

If you were homeless, as Johnny was, you could be invisible.

He had lived on the streets of Dublin for coming on five years, when London grew too rough and when he was sure no one in Ireland would remember him anymore. He found it easy to blend in with the rest of the community, to sink into the streets and to find his territory. He begged without seeming desperate. He drank tea and ate crappy sandwiches that people bought him instead of giving him money, because they thought he wanted drugs. But he was clean. He came back to Ireland clean, after a someone snuck him a few extra quid to get the ferry. He knew someone in London who'd kept his passport safe for him. It was out of date, now. He was here for life.

Being on the streets was worse than being in prison, except people felt sorrier for you. In prison, you got the food and the bed and the shelter, and when Johnny had been there he'd read a few books and he'd learned how to be something like a decent person. Getting out meant fighting for safety and losing weight and the constant temptation of an easy release from the pain and the mundanity and the constant seeking for human empathy.

Being on the streets meant dealing with drunkards and idiots and criticism, and trying to sleep when something was splashing about in the Liffey. He stood on the Quay to 'investigate'.

"Would ye shut up already?" he shouted. He was met by silence. "Bleedin' seagulls."

It was nights like this when the city's other natives were loud that Johnny wished he still drank. Sobriety was hell for an insomniac. He stared out over the Liffey, light dancing on its surface. He didn't know what time it was. Before half two, anyway. People hadn't been kicked out of the pubs, yet. They'd be worse than the birds.

A splash in the water below caught his attention. Something stared up at him, big eyes glowing in the dark, scaly skin with sharp teeth poking through a jagged smile.

"Who're you?" he asked, and the creature began to rise out of the water. From the waist up, it was like a man crossed with a lizard, though it mostly looked like it was made from the water it had been swimming in. Below the waist, dozens of long, thin tentacles pushed it upwards. A few stray arms grabbed at the bridge for support. "You're an ugly fecker, aren't you? Haven't seen something like you before."

There were many strange things in Dublin. A woman who sold emotion-changing fruit, a dog with wings that occasionally ate the seagulls that tried to eat people sandwiches - that was what Johnny's friend thought he'd seen, but he'd been high as a kite, then - and a few other odd occurrences that escaped the attention of the regular folk in town. But Johnny noticed, and this was different.

The lizard face grinned at him, eyes glistening. It almost looked like it was going to say something, when a tentacle wrapped around Johnny's leg. And another. And a third.

Together they lifted him, swinging him so suddenly he almost forgot to scream.

He was brought right within reach of the lizard's snapping mouth and sharp claws, and he couldn't fight. He was powerless.

All Johnny could do was scream as he was pulled at speed into the river, not loud enough to wake the other rough sleepers.

Dublin didn't notice.

Paul Carroll

Chapter One: Working Class Magic

Kurt Crane had barely slept. This is a typically true statement to make of the man. He was not what one would consider healthy, if health was measured by quality of life and counted the number of times a person died before they stayed that way. Kurt had lost track, but that was aside from the point.

Kurt's lack of sleep had more to do with an explosion of magical energy somewhere on his side of the globe. He was, unprofessionally, a magician, and previously a detective. He knew ancient magic, forbidden magic, new magic, new age magic, and classic magic, spoke more languages fluently than he was aware of, including both Latin and Pig Latin, and had, once upon a time, been cursed with a sort of immortality. He didn't know the full story, except that he always came back from the dead, born of a new mother, and he had become increasingly susceptible to changes in the magical world.

He nursed a headache that was like a hangover, but without the fun of drinking more than was advised, and significantly worse than Kurt was used to. It was more like a pneumatic drill at work in his head, if the drill was also exploding, a sensation that caused him no end of distress. He had been awake since two in the morning because of it, and didn't have a clue where to begin looking for it.

It was now past six in the morning, and the sun was rising. Kurt sat upright, looking at himself in the mirror. "I'm not doing it," he warned himself. "I'm not spending another lifetime working for other people."

He stood up in anger. His reflection did not join him.

"Don't give me that crap. I lost everything the last time. For once, just let me do my own thing." The reflection was silent. "What's my thing? I don't know, yet. That's not the point." The reflection kept its quiet, and Kurt shouted at it for another few minutes.

If he had slept for a little bit longer that night, or indeed over the past twenty-seven years, he might have remembered that the mirror was charmed to serve as a sounding board for problem solving. Sleep deprivation and a mild case of insanity combined, however, to point him in the direction of a one-sided argument that only the sudden desire for coffee could stop.

In most circles, one would say that the years had not been kind to Kurt. It was more accurate, in this case, to say that Kurt had not been kind to the years. Dying being something of an involuntary past-time for Kurt, he had abused his latest incarnation with years of inactivity in the professional sense.

He had lived many lives and accumulated what most would call 'an assortment of crap'. His wardrobe was stocked with articles of clothing from several centuries prior that held, among the countless protection charms that kept them in one piece all this time, sentimental value. Some of these were scattered across the floor.

His living room, study and kitchen - all the one space, by the landlord's insistence, even if Kurt had made that space slightly dimensionally transcendental - were filled with books from forgotten languages, some of which he had borrowed and forgotten to return for three centuries. He had books on demons, on ancient angelic lore, on all manner of magic and spell that one could think of, and at least a few dozen cookbooks mixed in for good measure. In a previous life, he had been a rather excellent cook. In this life, he suffered from impatience; fireballs did not supply heat at the right temperature or for the correct amount of time to properly cook anything suitable for eating.

Mid-coffee, while trying not to knock over a twelfth century text on either protecting against greater demon lords or making the perfect puffed pastry, he stopped to think. This was usually regarded as a bad idea. "Gods be damned. I have to reopen the office." The office existed in an extradimensional space, regarded unfavourably by the magical community for making local cats believe there was a ghost in the building. It was where Kurt had run his detective practice in the 1980s, before his untimely demise and the subsequent apathy for life that came with it.

He had once enjoyed being a detective. He liked helping people. Despite the problems the job that had brought him, it was the only thing he could think about doing right now. Just the idea of it made his headache subside slightly, like the universe's message was getting through so it could lay off shouting it at him.

"There's a case here," he said to himself. "Something is fundamentally wrong with the universe, and only Kurt Crane, Magical Detective can solve it. Not this hack who spends his days in sweatpants using his magic for his own personal amusement." He sighed heavily at the thought. "Big boy trousers on now, Kurt. Work to be done. A mystery to solve."

It was not a habit that Kurt liked, to talk to himself so much; he believed he had picked it up from his last mother, an Irish woman whose labours in cleaning were often accompanied by a full three-act one-woman play. He knew, once he hit the field, that he would need to stop his mutterings and musings and self-talks. He also knew that he would have to have a few words with himself about the journey to and from his office.

Most people with enough power to create an extradimensional office would have the foresight to create more than one doorway into it, a sort of shortcut to and from the office without needing to trudge across London and interact with, gods forbid, other people. Kurt was not one of those people. He had the power, and plenty more to boot, but hadn't thought when he'd made the office, that he would ever get bored with dealing with other people. And not just regular people: Londoners. On a one-to-one basis, Kurt could deal with them, but there were so many of them that staying indoors, in a burning building, was often preferable to making the trip across the road for something like bread or milk or the basic ingredients for summoning a lesser demon.

He thought about all of these things as he left his apartment through its front door, and not through, say, his fashionably unconscious wardrobe.

London did not necessarily have the best air in the world - though it used to be much worse, if anyone can believe that - but even then, it was fresh compared to Kurt's apartment. He would need to open a few windows, he thought, or completely remove the roof and every other floor above his own, just to air the place out.

It was early, which meant the Underground would be busier than usual and filled with more people than he had time for. He decided, instead, to try make a shortcut through a local park. The last vestiges of plant life in London were Kurt's cornerstones for staying relatively sane, not counting arguments with magical mirrors. His office was situated beside one, too, though it was smaller now than it had been when he'd set it up as a safehouse over a century ago.

His London was long gone, though it hadn't really been his London for a much longer time before that.

He tried not to think about what that meant, and instead climbed into a grove of trees that had been littered by local youths with cans and the occasional empty bottle of vodka so cheap it could be used as paint stripper. It would have to do.

Magic, as Kurt understood it, first began with trying to figure out what everything meant, and then trying to figure out what you meant. Intention was one of the most importantly elements of casting any sort of spell, be it a deadly fireball or a healing charm. The more a magician knew, the better. Knowledge truly was power.

Some spells no longer had symbols to guide them, and some never had any words to speak. As a groundskeeper approached Kurt's littered grove, positive he'd seen someone enter who was likely about to use it as a toilet, Kurt focused on the interconnectivity of plant life in the world. He pictured his office, and the little park in front of it, he channelled magic through his feet, careful not to burn his shoes in the process.

The earth swallowed him whole before the groundskeeper saw him. It also took the glass bottles and empty cans; if Kurt was going to make someone temporarily doubt their sanity, he was at least going to make their job a little bit easier for the day.

He was pleased with himself, until he was thrown violently into the air coming out the other side. That was the thing about teleportation spells. They could be sometimes unreliable. Still, taking the nature route was safer than direct teleportation, which would summon an army of bureaucrats and would-be soldiers to his location quicker than he could click his fingers.

"Bloody kids," he said to himself as a rain of empty cans of cheap lager fell down around him. He barely caught the glass bottles with what convention called telekinesis - what he had been taught was merely an extension of his will manifested by the invisible forces of the universe. It took him a few minutes to clean everything up, to crush the cans using his so-called telekinesis into an easier to collect cube, and to line up the bottles in such a way that they probably wouldn't break before they were picked up, and then he was on his way.

The office of Kurt Crane was situated in a residential building. It had not always been a building. For some time it had been a military camp. Before that, a small grove of trees. It was isolated and impossible to find unless you had real, agreed upon business with Kurt, or you were a cat.

He climbed the stairs to enter the building, when a woman erupted through the doors. She was in her late fifties, burdened with rubbish bags in both arms, and wearing a look of absolute determination. "You're a fresh face," the woman said to him. "Someone's nephew or something?"

He noticed a Letting sign outside the building. "Looking to move in, actually," he said to her. "Kurt Crane, ma-" He stopped himself. "May I help you with anything?"

She handed him a black sack. "Who says the youth of today are useless?"

"I do," Kurt told her, before realising it was both a rhetorical question, and a compliment of some vague description.

"I like you," she said laughing. "My name's Rose. I'm in 3a if you ever need anything. Assuming you move in." He walked with her to the curb. "You're not a weirdo, are you?"

"Not according to my mother," he responded. She turned to walk away from the building. "Not going back in?"

Rose chuckled. "Some of us still have to work to eat, young man. Maybe I'll see you around." She trotted off at her own pace - that is, slowly - and left Kurt to his own business.

This came as something of a relief to him. Kurt's office was also located in 3a, albeit in a pocket dimension that existed in the same space. He needed to use the same door as Rose had to enter the building, but step into one physical realm instead of another. Mostly this was done on instinct, and when he was sure he wasn't being watched, he disappeared from view.

He was barely capable of making the three flights of stairs before wanting to just blow the whole place up, but he felt apprehension played a bigger role there than physical fitness. He would work harder at both, he decided as he unlocked his office.

It still smelled like an old movie.

That is to say, Kurt had modelled his office around old detective movies, which included an unpleasant stale cigar stench that he needed to get rid of.

The books in the office, due to the endless amount of charms, spells and curses splattered across them, did not smell of cigar smoke, but they did occasionally growl at passers-by. They were similar, if not more dangerous, volumes to those in his apartment. Kurt kept them in the office in case of accidental demon gateways opening, at which point the dimension would collapse in on itself. Only the physical presence of Kurt could prevent that, and only if he cared enough to disrupt the failsafe.

Otherwise, the office was exactly as you'd expect a magical detective's office to look: filing cabinets that fit hundreds of years' worth of cases in them, a dusty desk that didn't have a computer, a coat rack with a jacket still hanging on it since the 1980s, and an assortment of magical items. He had a looking glass that could find any ship at sea, a comb that always brushed hair perfectly, a matchbox that never ran out of matches, and a pair of codebreaking glasses that didn't work on ancient magic.

He hated almost all of it, but couldn't justify changing anything.

A cloud of dust and time rose from the desk chair as he plonked himself down. He slammed a copy of The Black Pages on the desk, opening it where his ad usually sat - under

D for Detective - and clicked his fingers over the page. His old ad grew on the page, forcing other ads out of the way. The same thing would happen in every other copy of The Black Pages, much to the chagrin of the current editors, who thought they'd finally gotten rid of him.

"And now we play the waiting game," he said to himself.

There were a disproportionate number of people working as psychics and fortune tellers in Dublin. Peter Hughes was one of them. He was, he thought, at least a bit more approachable than most. He was well practiced in the art of being a communicable human being.

The one thing that Peter was not was legitimate, a fact that was true of almost every single psychic in the city. There was one woman who only did readings for her friends who could accurately predict the future, and a man just off George's Street who knew exactly when and how someone was going to die. Peter did not know about them. The entire magical community in Dublin was a mystery to him.

Instead, Peter was the sort of psychic who did a good job at reassuring people. His granny was convinced he was perfect for it. He was the seventh child of a seventh daughter, and the fact that he was gay, in her esteemed and verging on senile opinion, was enough for the spirits to give him a pass. That didn't make much sense to Peter, but he let it slide, and eventually took over his granny's spot at the gossip centre of Dublin in a small stall off Moore Street.

His current client was something of a regular. Her name was Missus Gillespie, and that was all she would ever tell him. She was in her seventies, a widow with children who'd practically abandoned her and grandchildren who wanted her money, and a great grandchild who thought she was scary looking. She knew who was behind on their bills, and who ate what for dinner every night, and when someone in Finglas was going to give birth, and who the illegitimate father was. She had all of the answers to everyone else's secrets, and paid Peter for the pleasure of listening to her go on at length, before asking for a palm reading.

"It's a lot of the same, Missus Gillespie. You're very old." They laughed at that. "Your money line looks good. I'd say get a scratch card, but I'm sure you already have a half dozen in your bag."

"And what about the life line?" she asked him. "Am I going to get cancer any time soon?"

He looked at her palm apathetically, and his vision blurred. He was watching her cross the road in something that felt like a dream. Liffey Street, he knew. He recognised it immediately. She shuffled across the road, completely unaware of the car speeding around the corner, the driver distracted and in a hurry. He crashed into her without slowing down, leaving poor old Missus Gillespie sprawled on the road.

He gasped out loud, and she looked at him with a fresh sort of terror. "That bad?"

"Jesus Missus Gillespie, I think you're going to die later," he told her.

"Ah feck off, Peter. This is just supposed to be a bit of fun." She looked at him, and the colour had gone from his face. "You're serious, aren't you?" Peter nodded. "Well what happens?"

He swallowed hard. "You're going to get hit by a car crossing the road on Liffey Street. Some time today, I think. The driver won't be paying attention, and you're too slow to avoid him yourself." He paused, letting go of her hands. "I'm really sorry, Missus Gillespie. I didn't mean to."

She dug her purse out of her handbag, pulling a fifty euro note loose. "Look, take that. If I die, my grandchildren don't deserve it. If I live, you can help me bring home my shopping next week. Deal?"

"Deal," he muttered, and watched Missus Gillespie leave his stall.

Peter's granny had, at one point, claimed she could see into the future. He hadn't believed it as being anything more the mad ramblings of an Irish granny, prone to hyperbole.

But maybe there was something more to it. Maybe, he thought, he had the Gift.

Missus Gillespie had been spooked, but these things do happen. She liked Peter. He was like his granny in a lot of ways. He held hands gently the way she did, but firm whenever they were scared. He could do palm readings and tea leaves and tarot cards, and he always knew the best thing to say. He helped her keep in touch with her children, and he helped her make the right decision about whether she should go to the cinema more often, or whether she should get a fancy TV package.

The Hughes family had been good to her, for a very long time, and she didn't want to hold it against Peter that he'd had a bit of a moment. He'd been teased a lot growing up, Missus Gillespie knew, because he was different. He didn't need that sort of treatment again.

"He's just trying to do his granny proud," Missus Gillespie decided. She left Marks, where she'd gotten herself a few nice bits for the kitchen for when her friends came over, fancy biscuits and some fresh bread, and crossed the Luas tracks. She'd made it a habit to walk around Dublin for a while before heading home to vegetate, having gone for the fancy TV package.

She barely realised when she'd reached Liffey Street, and was about to cross the road.

"It can't hurt to wait," she muttered.

The car came from Abbey Street, faster and more aggressive than any other driver in the city. He barely missed her, even as she stood on the path, and he made no attempt to stop. He turned onto the Quays, slowing only when a bus threatened to knock him to the side.

"Jesus, Mary and Joseph," Missus Gillespie said, blessing herself. "Peter Hughes is a bloody mystic."

Every great detective knew that you couldn't simply wait for answers to come to you. Kurt learned that from old movies. His phone, his only real connection to the modern world, was on standby for when - rather, if - someone wanted to hire him. In the meantime, he had a magical cataclysm to uncover, and no leads.

This wasn't just business. This was personal. This was a headache and a half, and almost no sleep.

So, he searched London. He went for an hour long walk, which didn't get him very far, before deciding that he was looking in all the wrong places and in all the wrong ways. If he had practiced with his magic just a little bit more over the last twenty-odd years, he might have been able to figure it out more easily. Instead, he needed outside help. The sort of help that existed only outside the regular laws of Space and Time.

There was a Door. There were probably several of them, but Kurt knew of one in particular, pale green and scratched up and a little bit burned when a frustrated wizard had thrown a fireball at it ten years ago. It was known as the Floating Door, and it led to the Impossible Place. Kurt was not a fan of the names, but they had stuck over the years.

The Floating Door did not appear regularly. Sometimes it would only pretend to appear, to make unsuspected wizards and magicians fall into the Thames. It didn't always appear in London, but that had been a preferred spot for some time now.

It stood, or floated, before him now, right in the middle of Piccadilly. No one else seemed to have noticed it. More to the point, no one else seemed to have noticed him, and he was currently holding a fireball in his hand.

That's enough Mister Crane.

The voice was wooden, though Kurt had never been sure whether it was the Door or the occupant speaking. It didn't matter. It had smashed into his brain like a warhead. He lowered the fireball all the same, and watched the Door open.

The Impossible Place was dark. When the Door shut, there was no way out. It simply disappeared. It had no floor, though that didn't seem to make walking any more difficult. Gravity felt at odds with itself, holding him on a relative plane. It ached to walk. Every muscle in his body was tense from the effort. He suddenly remembered why he didn't like coming here.

He took a deep breath, and thought back to his last visit. A strengthening spell filled his body, and he no longer felt like he was going to crushed into a cube. "Thank you for seeing me," Kurt said as loud as he could.

Immediately in front of him, a woman turned around. She had not appeared to be there before. She had, Kurt knew, four eyes. She always had at least two closed, either the two that looked right at him, her birth eyes, or the two that she had earned. One was on her forehead, the other on the back of her skull, where the hair had to brushed away so that she could See.

Her name was Madame Madness, and the Impossible Place was hers.

"You look like crap, Kurt," she told him without hesitation. "It used to be that if you wanted to visit me, you'd just show up. Greatest magician in the world, begging for help."

"It's been a rough lifetime."

"Bull. You just didn't want to do anything with it but vandalise my Door. What, because I wouldn't help some grieving teenager with his decades old lady issues?" She almost smiled at him. "You think you ought to have seen this coming? I'm the one with Absolute Sight, Kurt, not you. Oh, you're strong when you're not rusty, but some of us had to get by in other ways."

He sat down. He didn't mean to, but suddenly there was a chair behind him and it was too inviting to resist. They were in a café in Paris.

The Impossible Place always made his head spin. He tried not to let the spell he'd cast waiver.

"I know you exist outside of the other world, but you must have felt the same disturbance I did," he said to her.

"Straight to business, as always. No time for catching up, eh?" She drank from a cocktail made from fire. "I felt it. The Door wanted to leave London, but this is my city. Something is happening now, and something else might happen."

"Might?"

This time she smirked, and looked down at him from a throne made of swords. They were on a television set. "Time is a mess, Kurt. People think it's like a river, but they ignore the way it splits and overspills. They ignore the whirlpools in the lakes where the river is disturbed. They ignore the Source and the Sea." She closed her regular eyes, and her forehead eye looked at him. "It is my job to monitor, Kurt, and to stay out of the narrative."

He had been through this before. "I still need your help."

"You want the same thing you were looking for ten years ago, Kurt. You want the Mind's Eye. Tell me, will you use it to try find a way to fix your old mistakes?"

He shook his head, and paused. "Only if they're connected to what I felt this morning. Something broke, Madame. I intend to fix it."

They sat in a hovel in London, centuries into the past. Kurt had lived there, once upon a time.

"The Eye is difficult, and can only be worn once in a lifetime. Even by you. When it feels you have done your job, it will leave you. Do you understand?"

"I get it. No looking for answers I'm not meant to have."

She drank from a chipped cup. Dirty water. She didn't seem to care. "You will be burdened twice. The first will be a loss of a sense. It is a security deposit. It will return when the Eye leaves. If you break the rules, you'll never get it back. Do you understand?" He nodded. "I need a verbal answer, Kurt."

"I understand, Madame." He didn't know how he'd solve the case blind, but he didn't have time to think about that. He needed the Eye. "What's the other burden?"

She tapped the side of her head. "A loss of senses. Over time. Solve your case quickly Kurt, or the Eye will take its toll. And it won't give you anything back. Do you understand?"

He nodded again. "I understand. Work quickly, solve the case, get rid of the Eye."

"Good. One more thing. I don't want you visit me before you die again. It distresses me to see you like this." She didn't give him a choice before she touched him for the first time, placing the palm of her right hand on his forehead. "Good luck Kurt. Something tells me you're going to need it."

There was a brief burning sensation, before he was catapulted back into London. Night had fallen outside the Impossible Place.

The Mind's Eye flared, invisible to the outside world but showing him a whole other layer to reality. Across the sea, Kurt knew, something was happening.

Chapter Two: The Mourning After the Night Before

The thing about dreams that no one realises, the thing about the really gruesome ones with monsters in them, and the sort with people dying, is that usually they actually happened. Kurt knew this. He didn't like it. It was detrimental to his sleep patterns to wake up from a dream about three homeless men being savagely killed by a monster with the claws of a dinosaur and the tentacles of an octopus, if it still counted when there were dozens of tentacles.

He had not enjoyed the dream one bit, anyway, but knowing that it was true made it all the worse. He blamed the Mind's Eye. He'd barely gotten to bed when he'd had the dream and seen this new sort of terrible monster striking from the dark waters of an unknown river.

No, that wasn't necessarily true, he realised. He hadn't *seen* the monster. He'd *been* the monster. He'd tasted the flesh of the men, one of them so filled with alcohol that Kurt had gotten slightly drunk from the act. Another was so filthy that his skin had to be mulched and discarded. The third was just right, fresh and healthy.

None of them knew what was coming. None of them knew the other had been attacked. Over the space of an hour, an hour Kurt couldn't burn from his mind, the monster had eaten all three men.

Then the world exploded.

Not literally, of course, but it felt that way in Kurt's head. First euphoria through the dream, then his previous headache dialled up to eleven. He found himself screaming, and it took a conscious effort to stop.

"What the bloody hell was that?" he asked himself. His sheets were soaked, and he wasn't entirely sure it was sweat. Dirt and leaves clung to the bedsheets. He didn't think he'd gone to bed like that.

This was, he knew, something magical. Sometimes he hated magic.

He showered, which took longer than he wanted it to. He was covered in grime, like he'd been swimming in the river the whole time. When he saw himself in the mirror, his whole body tense, he sighed. There was a time when he thought that maybe he was in good physical health, for a man who kept dying. Reincarnation and a soul made from magic had a way of reconstructing the same body over and over again, albeit from birth. Always the same Kurt, impossible to keep down.

He was sore from his time with Madame Madness. The Impossible Place was a nightmare to sit around in for an extended duration. It was like a full-body workout, which he hadn't quite scheduled.

"There are worse things, I suppose," he said to himself, and dried off instantly. Towels were something of a comfort item for Kurt, who was capable of magically drying himself with a thought. Of all the things he'd practiced during his current lifetime, that was his favourite.

It was still early, so he sat down to meditate. He did not do this often. Or, he realised, at all. This was a habit from a past life. He closed his eyes, trying not to think he'd wasted twenty years, and tried to remember the dream.

He didn't know the people. He knew that much immediately. Dreams were usually filled with people one knew in their daily lives, someone they'd seen on the street or the bus, or someone they'd worked with at some point. Kurt remembered faces.

The men were all homeless, he thought. Homeless, poor, scared, and dead. He tried to think about the monster, but there was nothing there to think about. He didn't know what it had done to the men aside from eating them.

So he focused in the river. He didn't know it, which wasn't a surprise. There were a lot of rivers in the world. He had a vague, flickering notion of a bridge, white railed and arching over the water, but that was it before he was pulled from his meditation by a phone call.

He looked at the time. Seven in the morning. He thought maybe he'd fallen asleep again.

"Hello?" he said weakly into the phone.

"Is this Kurt Crane? I need your help. I saw your ad in the Black Pages. I kept thinking about calling, and it never felt like a good idea, but I'm getting desperate."

Kurt sighed, deliberate and slow. "Start from the beginning. What's your name?"

"Edward. Edward Armstrong. I... I didn't even believe in magic until yesterday, and now it's all I can think about." That didn't add up, but Edward continued. "I just *found* The Black Pages. I was looking for help, and I found you."

It had been a long time since someone had said that to Kurt. He almost laughed. "Kid, you have no idea how long I've been waiting to hear that."

"Thirty years, give or take," Edward responded. "Which is weird, because you don't sound that old." Kurt paused. "Something is happening to me, Mister Crane, and I think someone wants to kill me because of it."

This was exactly the sort of case that Kurt had been hoping for. Insane. Exciting. With a client who needed him. This was perfect.

"Tell you what, we should meet first. You can tell me everything face to face."

"Baker Street," Edward said firmly. "That's where you wanted to meet, right?" He didn't wait for a response, or a time, when he hung up.

"Well actually, yes," Kurt said quietly to the room. "I think I'm going to like this job."

A moment of panic hit him when he realised he probably needed to leave his apartment immediately, given Edward's complete lack of meeting time. He grabbed a messenger bag that had been hanging by a hook on his wall for a year, untouched, and began stuffing it with everything he thought he might need, but wasn't sure he'd ever use. He had a notebook that never filled up, a pen that never ran out, a small crystal ball that glowed red whenever someone told a lie, a coat that could fold to the size of his palm without creasing, and an umbrella handle that could turn into a full-sized golf umbrella with a flick of movement, and he wasn't sure he had used any of them in a lifetime or two.

He stood in front of the mirror in his living room - a straightforward piece, lacking in any sort of magic - and assessed himself. His hair was scruffy, and always would be. He stood upright. He'd taken to dressing like a hipster, he realised with a tinge of regret, but there was nothing to be done about that now.

"You can do this," he told himself. "It's just the job. The same one you've done over and over again." He took a few deep breaths, and tried to channel magic through his body. It took a moment, to feel the familiar tingle in his fingertips, and the effort activated the Mind's Eye for a moment. Otherwise he felt confident that he could perform on command, should the occasion arise.

He had learned a long time ago that there was no telling what sort of mess he would accidentally walk into while working a case. Whether it was vampires, witches, demons or his ex, there was always something out there inclined to cause him a fatal injury.

Peter Hughes really ought to have seen it coming, but it took him by surprise when Missus Gillespie reappeared at his stall the next day. He was partly surprised because she only ever showed up once a week, and partly surprised that she was still alive.

"You did it," she said to him. "You actually did it." She hugged him tightly, her tiny body frail and bony. "I was crossing the road yesterday and I remembered what you said. And look: I'm not dead!"

The fortune teller's face turned bright red. "You have no idea how relieved I am to hear that." He didn't know how to treat it gently, so he decided to ask outright, "Was it exactly as I described?"

"Everything except me dying at the end, because I didn't step off the path," she replied. "Jesus, where's my head?" She reached into a carrier bag - a staple part of the Irish Granny wardrobe - and pulled out a box of donuts. Dublin was, in those days, full to the brim with donuteers, so Peter wasn't convinced she had had to go to any significant effort for him. That put his mind at ease. "I didn't know what you liked. Only one of us is psychic." She laughed at her own joke.

Peter did not laugh, aside from a sort of polite chuckle that could almost be mistaken for choking. He took the donuts from her uneasily. "You didn't have to do this," he said to her.

"Don't be silly," she said with a wave of her hand, her whole body more relaxed and casual than anybody had any right to be following a near death experience. "Look, you're single right?" She laughed again. Peter almost crushed the donut box in his hands at the sound of her. "I want to set you up with one of my kids. I have eight, but I think a few are the wrong gender for you."

He placed the donuts down on the table to prevent himself from obliterating them, and tried to remain calm. "And are any of the others actually gay, Missus Gillespie, or are you just trying to thank me?" She didn't have a response. "Look, I'm genuinely glad you're not dead, and thanks a million for the donuts. But I don't need to be set up on a date. Maybe a gym membership when I'm done with these."

She stared back blankly so he started fake laughing at his own joke. Eventually she joined in. By the time she left him alone, Peter was sure his eyes were going to roll back so far he'd see his brain.

If he'd known she'd react like that, he thought, he might have let her get hit by the car.

Still, it was a success. He had seen the future, and changed it. Now, he just needed to figure out how to make a living from his newfound gift. Maybe it was the fake crystal ball, or the tarot cards, or the velvet curtains, but he didn't think 'Peter Hughes: Actual Psychic' was going to help him strike rich.

London air, Kurt realised, had a smell. He couldn't quite place it, not anymore, with his own nose no longer performing its duties, but the absence hit him hard when he reached Baker Street.

He wouldn't have minded so much if the Mind's Eye had been in any way useful since he'd acquired it. Maybe, he thought, he needed it for Edward's case. It was unlikely. Cases of stalkers rarely resulted in something coming from an otherwise unseen plane of reality. Usually it was a regular infatuation, or a vampire, or an aroused werewolf, or a demon. Once or twice, a ghost. But every time he'd been able to identify the problem without the use of the Mind's Eye.

He spied a café across the road, part of a chain, and realised he'd never arranged to meet Edward at a specific location. Still, he reasoned, if Edward knew he wanted to go to Baker Street, he might also know he'd want to go to the café.

He just hoped that Edward didn't bring up the reason Kurt liked Baker Street so much. It felt obvious to Kurt, of course, but the thought still embarrassed him. He had always been a fan of Sherlock Holmes stories. He loved the mystery and the intrigue and the normal answer to the complexity of the case. He aspired to be the next Sherlock Holmes, not just because Holmes was a legend, renowned and highly regarded. Holmes was free. Holmes was fictional. Holmes wasn't on the run from the Powers That Be for breaking the fundamental laws that govern the universe.

Kurt looked to the sky uneasily before entering the café. The Mind's Eye didn't reveal any hidden dangers to him, so he sat down at a table by himself.

It took only a few seconds for him to be joined. The man had come straight from the register, two cups and a plate in his hands.

"Just in time," the man said. "I'm Edward. I thought you might be hungry, since you haven't eaten in a while."

"How did you-" Kurt began, only to be interrupted by his own stomach growling at him. "Oh, I like you."

"It's just one of those stuffed croissant things they do here. And a tea. Two sugars, bit of milk." Edward passed the cup along, and waited for a response of some description from Kurt. "You're not freaked out?"

Kurt shrugged. "Kid, I've seen it all already. But usually psychics… are you psychic? Anyway, usually they hate me too much to buy me breakfast."

Edward Armstrong seemed, for the first time, taken aback. "I'm older than you," Edward noted. "That doesn't seem right. I thought you were going to be this old man. Like, ancient."

"You wouldn't be wrong," Kurt said casually. "Dying brings out the youth in people." He took a bite from the croissant. He could still taste, which was confusing, but nothing tasted quite the same, like the flavours were put in in the wrong order. "This is really good, thank you."

The other man stared back at him blankly. "Jesus. Am I going to get you killed?"

"Everyone wonders that," Kurt said casually, though it wasn't true. With Edward being his first case in a long time, no one had almost gotten Kurt killed recently but him.

Edward shook his head, his hands shaking and his eyes tightly shut. "No, I can practically see it. It's all my fault. I shouldn't have-"

He jumped to his feet, his chair screeching on the floor, and Kurt grabbed his hand. He applied just enough force that Edward wouldn't slip away, trying to be a calming force for a man who clearly had too much on his mind. "No one gets me killed but me," Kurt said to him. "Whatever you're worried is going to happen, I'm sure it's because of this stalker issue you're having."

With all eyes on him, Edward sat down quietly. "Really?"

"Really," Kurt assured him. "Now stay put for a second. Got a little trick to pull off to keep attention away from us. You keep jumping up out of your seat like that and we'll get nothing discussed."

He planted his hands on the table, willing them some peace and privacy. Distractions floated into the air like flies, invisible to everyone but Kurt and Edward, and even for them they were gone in an instant. It was something he had learned a long time ago, and abused to no end as a pickpocket, and he had always found it helpful in the interim when discussing sudden apocalyptic scenarios with people who could loosely be described as friends.

"There," he said proudly. "Haven't done that in a while, but there we go. We can talk freely." With that, he placed his notebook and pen on the table, with the crystal ball beside them. "Two for taking notes, one for catching lies," he explained. "Gotta know what I'm up against, you know?"

Edward nodded. "I didn't think it would be like this," he admitted. "I thought we would go to your office, but all I kept thinking was Baker Street."

"This is better. My office is a kip." He clicked the pen. "A series of simple questions, Edward, just to rule out some possibilities. Are you ready?"

There was no waiting for a response from Edward. The questions were all that mattered. When Kurt asked him if he had been approached by a pale man or woman at any point in the last few days, Edward had to point out that they were in London, and even in the summer paleness was a common feature. So Kurt rephrased, to include any potential desire said person might have for drinking blood or eating human flesh. At this point, Kurt could conclude that Edward was not the target of a vampire, a ghoul, or a shapeshifter.

When asked if he had had dreams about someone of his sexual preference - most likely a woman, regardless - flying through his bedroom window at night, Edward tried his utmost best to mask his embarrassment. British sensibilities dictated that talk of the bedroom avoid cafés on Baker Street. "Just answer, please," Kurt said with some impatience.

"No, nothing unusual," Edward grumbled.

"Not a succubus, then," Kurt concluded.

Edward guffawed. "Mr Crane, I know I'm new to all of this, but are these questions necessary?"

Kurt shrugged with disaffection. "If you'd rather I leave it to chance and be unable to save you from one creature of the night or another, we can close the book on this immediately. I refuse to go into this unprepared." Edward looked bashfully at the table. "Ignorance can lead to death,

Edward. Mine or yours. Will you let me do my job properly?"

There was a flicker in Edward Armstrong's eyes, a sort of recognition of truth that he'd been afraid of looking for. "That's what happened to you, isn't it? You really did die."

"Many times," Kurt admitted. "Hurts like heck, but I always come back. Hijack a womb without my consent or the mother's, born the same baby every time. Sometimes my mothers were barren to begin with, and I'm a blessing. Other times, they were already pregnant and I took over. No choice in the matter."

"That's horrible," Edward whispered.

"And it's why I'd rather not die again any time soon. There's no telling who I'm keeping from the world by showing up again."

Edward seemed to understand, though he was confused why Kurt hadn't opened with his next question: had Edward disturbed the forces of a Lord or Lady of Darkness? Being a man of simple taste and small ambition, it seemed absurd. He didn't have a notion who or what Kurt had been asking about. The detective assured him that it was probably for the best that he didn't know.

Whether intentionally or accidentally, Edward had also not attempted to summon a demon since the last full moon. He wasn't sure how, he said, at which point Kurt told him that it was a bit like trying to raise the dead but you removed as much protection as possible. That, or you use specific rituals and lots of blood. Kurt was not fond of either method.

"Are we almost done?" Edward asked.

"Almost," Kurt told him. His client was shifting in his seat. They hadn't been there for very long. Kurt was only a quarter of the way through his tea and barely a few bites into his breakfast. "Have you eaten or otherwise consumed something unnatural or supernatural in the last twenty four hours?"

Edward sighed. "Does processed food count?"

"Almost all food is processed," Kurt told him. "Think a little more outside the box."

"Then no, nothing weird."

Kurt grinned savagely. "Weird is subjective, Mr Armstrong. Supernatural is normal to many more people than you realise." Edward nodded in response. His face had been stripped of all colour. "You look like you need to throw up," Kurt noted.

"I just don't want to be here anymore than I have to," Edward told him. "Next question, please."

Kurt tried a calming spell on Edward, and it recoiled. His agitation, whatever was causing it, was too great for simple magic to help. "Last question, Edward. Have you recently met anyone strange who might want to cause you either undue harm or excessive pleasure?"

"Do you count?"

"I'm just here to keep you alive and put your mind at ease. Not me."

"Then no," Edward said with a grimace. "What does this mean?"

Kurt looked at his notes. "It means you're not being hunted by a monster, you're not the target of a demon, you're not cursed by an old god, you're not tied up in a supernatural contract, and you're not in immediate danger." He closed his notebook with some pride. "We'll monitor things for the next few days. It might just be a regular person with a regular infatuation."

"And if it isn't?" Edward asked. His eyes were flicking towards the door. "I feel like I'm drowning, Mr Crane. What if it's not a regular person?"

Kurt downed the rest of his tea. It had gone just cool enough to drink. "Then you can count your blessings that one of the most powerful magicians in London is sitting across the table from you."

That seemed of little comfort to Edward, who immediately darted from the café and emptied his stomach onto the path. He did not return.

Chapter Three: The World Yet to Come

Following his meeting with Edward Armstrong, Kurt was left with more questions on top of his answers. It seemed strange to him, to even the walking oddity of a man that was Kurt Crane, that someone could have contacted him for help who was not in immediate danger. There was a certain magical prerequisite to seeing Kurt's advertisement in the Black Pages. He knew that he would need to figure it out sooner than later, and uncover the mystery of Edward's knowledge of his preferences.

In the meantime, he had the Mind's Eye to concern himself with. Madame Madness had been quite clear: the longer he held onto the Eye, the worse it would be. He needed to use it to find that which couldn't be seen, and put a stop to whatever was breaking the laws of the universe, before he was ripped of whatever sanity he had remaining.

The problem was that Baker Street felt wrong. His feet brought him to the Underground, where a wave of his hand over the ticket scanner opened the barrier for him. He didn't usually carry much by way of money, largely down to not having any, and he wasn't about to waste it.

He hopped into the Bakerloo line, heading south, his feet operating on autopilot. The Mind's Eye was like playing a game, with someone else controlling his movements. He stood, rather than sat in one of a few empty seats, because the Eye made him. He ran from the carriage the moment they reached Waterloo, unsure what the problem was, and only stopped running when he hit the fresh air.

He collapsed against a wall and slid to the floor. "What was that all about?" he asked himself, and tried to think about what the Eye might have seen that he hadn't.

No monsters. No one with magic. He would have sensed them anyway. One old woman. Three teenagers. One civil servant.

Her.

He thought about her. Perfect posture, but tense. A badge clipped to her jacket. At first glance, nothing special. Just an access card. But there, a flicker of a spell.

"Damage Control," he whispered to himself. The bureaucracy, policing and marketing agency of the magical community worldwide. As a governing body, they hated Kurt. Partially it was because of what he could do, and partially it was because of what he couldn't help but do. Mostly it was because he was too good at avoiding them.

It wasn't unusual to see them in public, though the coincidence of timing didn't escape him. Then again, he reasoned, he might have simply picked up some of Edward's paranoia. He never usually worried about Damage Control these days. He had, for the most part, been quiet the last few years. Sure, every now and then he and a couple of friends got together to stop some Big Bad or another, but they never caused too much structural damage. It wasn't like the Great Fire of London, or wiping a whole town of demonically possessed people and their cult-born demon spawn from the face of reality. The worst he'd done lately was, maybe, sink a ship or raise a building, or aid the escape of a wanted fugitive. But that was it.

He tried to be calm, but it wasn't working.

"What was it Madame Madness said about the Mind's Eye?" he asked himself. "Something about sanity."

And maybe, he realised, the woman hadn't been Damage Control. Maybe the Eye was toying with him.

He couldn't be certain, of course. He was used to being right all the time, but that was usually retrospectively and after some considerable time gathering evidence to prove his point.

As chance would have it, while Kurt approached the Thames, he had been right. He wouldn't know for sure, not for a while, because the woman on the Underground hadn't noticed him, but she had come from Damage Control on an assignment. The stress of it had kept her uptight, and the mounting pressure to do this one job correctly had caused her to miss her stop. By the time she reached Waterloo station again, Kurt would be long gone.

He looked into the water, and all memory or concern regarding her slipped away. The Mind's Eye was at work, showing him something he didn't believe was possible. This was a peculiar notion for a man like Kurt to have, he knew, and soon he would be over it. In the meantime, he stared open-mouthed into the river at a magical symbol that simply floated under the water as if carved in a fixed location in space-time.

"Now what do we have here?" he asked himself, perhaps a bit too loudly, drawing the attention of an old man trying to feed ducks that would never land nearby.

Kurt pulled out his notebook and pen, and started sketching. The symbol looked old, or maybe new - sometimes it was hard to tell - and not at all like anything he'd ever stumbled upon in his studies. This was perhaps the most troublesome aspect about it. Kurt had read hundreds of books on magic, magical symbols, magical practices and magical potential, and none of them suggested that something like this was possible. And, as far as he was concerned, none of them contained the symbol. He would need to check what remained of his records, of course, but that would come later.

He wasn't sure of the connection to Edward, but he thought that maybe it would be important in the grand scheme of thing. He almost hoped it might point him in the right direction for his other case, that of the broken laws of the universe, but that would require a headache and more to get through, and he wasn't sure the Mind's Eye was going to let him last that long.

The Mind's Eye nagged at him to look upwards, and he followed the river. More symbols were etched into the water's currants, unmoving as the river poured towards the sea.

He walked for a good half hour, keeping an eye out for the symbols, all of them identical, before crossing the river. More of the same symbol were on the other side.

Whatever they meant, he didn't like it. There was power in them. And, he shuddered at the idea, they were set up like a runway of sorts. Whatever the symbols were for, whatever spell was being crafted in the Thames, it was going to mean bad news for whoever was caught in it. He thought about the boats that routinely travelled up and down the river, and all the people who lived and worked along the waterside. Worst case scenarios were easy when you understood the dangers.

This was something new. This was something Kurt had never faced before, or stopped before, and he wasn't sure his questions to Edward were going to make this any more clear. Someone, or something, was up to something in London, and Kurt reasoned that he was the only one in any position to stop it.

London was his city, always, and he would be damned if a second-rate wizard with a knack for writing magic into water was going to take that from him.

This was war.

Peter Hughes had a problem, and a blank lottery ticket.

The problem was a moral one: would it be cheating to look into the future in order to win the Lotto? It seemed simple. But then he thought about all the good he could do with the money, and that seemed like a balance. Imagine, he thought, someone who knew they were going to win the jackpot already knowing how best to divide the money for the maximum benefit of everyone.

Imagine getting to buy his own house.

That second thought stalled him, for just a moment. "What's the worst that could happen?" he asked. It was a rhetorical question, at first, until he remembered that he could actually answer it himself. "Future vision," he said with delight.

The important thing to remember about seeing the future is that it is rarely as exciting as one expects it to be. Peter had seen the horror of a client and family friend dying, and that had so far been too much.

When he closed his eyes to try force his newfound power to work, he was met by distress in snapshots, an unclear future unfolding before him. Success in his plan. The jackpot. A new house - his *dream* house. His friends and family over to celebrate. Everyone wanting money for something. Arguments. A fist fight. Lots of crying. Lots of alone time. Snapshots. A pounding at his door. A man, a woman, and a monster made from an oak tree. *Ent*. The word screamed at him. Trying to run, but blocked inside. *Damage Control.* Misuse of magic. Theft. Arrest. An infinite dungeon.

He was crying when the visions stopped. "That's no good at all," he whimpered, and crashed down onto the floor.

There was a whole world out there that he knew nothing about, that his new ability was opening him up to in a forceful, lonely way. He didn't know who Damage Control were, but he knew he didn't want anything to do with them if he could help it.

He needed an alternative. He needed to be less conspicuous. He needed to win less than the jackpot. So he tried again, wiping his eyes dry. Once again, everything came in snapshots. Collecting his winnings. A party. A new house, smaller. A holiday. A fight with his family. Nothing too drastic. Until someone throws a phone book on his table. *The Black Pages.* Other fortune tellers. Someone knows the truth. Someone threatens to expose him.

"No good," he said to himself, crashing back into the present. He didn't know *The Black Pages*, either, but it seemed inherently less detrimental to his health than Damage Control. He scribbled down a note to try find a copy, and dove into round three of Future Vision.

Snapshots. Winning a smaller amount again. A few thousand. Something to live off. A deposit on a house, maybe. A night out with friends. No arguments, except about who's dating who. No questions about his abilities. No suspicion. No blackmail. No Damage Control. No mysterious phone books. Just a small slice of happiness.

He filled in the numbers on his lottery slip, and immediately left for a nearby newsagents to play, before he could change his mind.

Though it was a small act, it was one that would open him up to greater dangers than he'd been willing to let himself see.

The symbols in the Thames led Kurt to the one person he hadn't expected to see again that day: Edward Armstrong.

His client was out for a walk - or he was simply afraid to sit still anywhere, it was hard to tell. He was wholly oblivious to Kurt's presence. This was the perfect opportunity, the detective realised, to try find the person who'd been following Edward. But to do that, Kurt couldn't be seen. He summoned up some distractions again, and kept his distance from the other man, keeping an eye out for anything unusual. The Mind's Eye whirred, and he was uncomfortably aware of its attempts to find something where there was nothing: a stalker.

"I'm wasting my time," he grumbled, though he kept pace with Edward nonetheless. It was a boring and uneventful route. Edward was shifty the entire time, constantly looking over his shoulder. That was the thing about paranoia, Kurt noted, there was no telling when a feeling of being followed was the genuine article or a trick of the mind.

Edward broke into a sprint at some point, moving quicker than Kurt had given him credit for. But the magician didn't need magic to keep up. He ran, light on his feet and swift as ever, keeping up with the older man easily. He kept to the shadows and the bushes, ducking out of view whenever he felt his distraction spell wavering and barely feeling the need to rest.

The same couldn't be said for his client. Edward leaned over, hands on his knees, and emptied his stomach. That was twice - twice too many times - that Kurt had seen Edward do this. There was something pitiable about seeing someone throw up in public, whether you knew them or not. Human compassion brought upon feelings of guilt and an emphatic desire to help.

That was why Kurt wondered if he even classified as being human anymore, or if his repeated and painful deaths had robbed him of some basic qualities of life. He was a shadow of himself, cast by a dozen different lights, stretched thin across the ground in whatever direction he landed.

He watched Edward recover from his anxiety, though not the paranoia, and continue his walk through the streets of London as if nothing had happened, and he felt nothing.

Edward was just another blink of an eye in the grand scheme of things, mortal and impermanent and doomed for the same fate as just about every other person in Kurt's life.

But he was also a pay check, so Kurt followed him, keeping an eye out for something or someone who might wish the poor man harm.

They passed the river three or four times on Edward's walk, and Kurt reasoned that maybe he was just trying to wear himself out, so that he could possibly sleep that night with everything running through his mind. It's what Kurt would have done, if Kurt ever had trouble clearing his mind, but it didn't make it any more frustrating to follow the same path until the sun began to set.

Edward threw up again before heading home, locking his door with a few distinct clicks. Kurt could hear him from outside, a charm cast to carry the sounds a little bit better. When he was satisfied that Edward was staying in for the night, he laid an alarm in the area. If anything magical passed through, Kurt would know. It was the least he could do for Edward. Some sort of early warning system. He could call him. He could find a way to reach him quickly. He could at least figure out what was happening to his client that had him so disturbed. And, when all the goodness in the world would inevitably fail, he could remind himself that Edward was going to be paying him.

The walk home felt a bit better, after that. "Maybe I just needed the fresh air," he said to himself. "A good long walk. A little bit of magic. A few different spells." He hadn't felt this much like himself in a long time. All that said, he still wished he could just teleport home. Damage Control and the Powers That Be had certainly put a dampener on that aspect of his life. There was simply no freedom in being a recluse.

Eventually he reached his apartment, taking a stack of letters up the stairs with him and collapsing into his favourite chair. A bill. A reminder of a bill. A local politician looking for votes, not realising that Kurt wasn't registered. And a couple of actual letters.

One he discarded almost immediately in the sort of broken hearted fashion that he assumed, incorrectly, all teenage girls had mastered. The other he stared at with suspicion for a few minutes before opening it.

Kurt,

I don't know if this will reach you, or when. I had to raise a few uncooperative spirits just to get this address. Things are going down over here that need your less than gentle touch. Gary didn't want me to write, but I think we're in over our heads.

I can get you safe passage, free from watching eyes. Gary will give you some cover while you're here, to act a little more freely.

Please Kurt, I think this one is going to take the three of us. We always were good together. Give me a call. My number's the same. I'm still in the phone book.

Your friend,
Arnold.

Kurt put the letter down. It had been a year or more since he'd heard from Arnold Schultz, a part-time necromancer and full-time asshole as far as Kurt was concerned. And a true friend. Even if he had developed certain American tendencies.

"Crap," he muttered. "Bad timing, Arnold. Really bad timing." He didn't have a choice. He'd have to ignore it for the time being.

Arnold and Gary were two of the best at what they did, even if no one knew they did it. Together they were a dangerous group, to themselves and others. One seasoned magician, one dreaded necromancer, and one Reaper charged with collecting both of their souls, instead working with them to stop certain Undesirables from breaching their reality.

He missed his friends, sometimes, when he let himself relax a bit and emote. If he wasn't in the middle of a case, and if he wasn't currently wearing the Mind's Eye to deal with an explosion of magical power on his own side of the world, he'd be joining them.

He looked at the other letter again, and decided against reading it. Some parts of his past were best left sealed until he wasn't on the job.

"Soon," he told himself, and tucked it away on his bookshelf beside half a dozen others just like it.

He lay down in bed, head spinning with ideas and vibrant humanity, and he tried to shut it all out. He tried to focus on the job, and on the catastrophe he was sure he had to prevent.

He might have dreamed that night, of the girl whose letters he never opened, of the friends who needed him, if he hadn't been overcome by a sense of magical dread as his eyes began to drift shut. Whether it was the Mind's Eye or his own magical perception returning to him like muscle memory, he knew that something bad was going to happen again, and he remained powerless to do anything about it.

Chapter Four: Wayward Wizards

The water was wild with movement beneath its surface as the beast that had failed to make the headlines stirred from the closest thing to slumber it would know. Kurt watched it, hovering above a river that wasn't his own, like a ghost hanging haunting over a bed. It took him a few moments, as much as dreamtime respected the concept of time, to figure out where he was.

"Dublin," he whispered. He had been to the city before, a long time ago by some people's standards. He'd been a child in the 90s, returning to a home that was never his. His mother's home. A runaway Irish girl. He knew the river and the sounds of the people and the way they understood humour and death, and he knew their myths and their stories and their love of telling stories that seemed to go nowhere if you didn't listen long enough.

He recognised the river from old photographs of his mother's. He recognised the bridges and the buildings and a few shopfronts that hadn't changed in years, like the comic shop he'd hidden in that made him realise he didn't need to be a hero just because he had powers.

And something moved under the surface of the Liffey that had never been there before.

It rose. First a head breached the surface, almost like a lizard's. No, he thought, a dinosaur. Or a monster movie creature from a million years ago, buried beneath the crust of the Earth until it was ready to eat again.

It was bigger than he thought it would be, big enough to consume half a man in one bite. He had a memory of it, a memory built into a dream that he couldn't quite grasp anymore, and it wasn't this large. It didn't have this many teeth, and its eyes weren't this aware, and he hadn't been so frightened by it. Now it wasn't just new and undefined in its ferociousness. Now it was big enough to put up a fight.

Its monster movie lizardman body stopped at the waist, where it became a tentacled beast from the deepest depths of the ocean, hundreds of slimy arms thrashing about as it awoke from stillness. They wrapped around a bridge - the Ha'penny Bridge, Kurt remembered - and helped the creature see further out of the banks of the river as it hefted itself up.

It was part made from water, where it still made contact with the Liffey. Some of its scales were transparent, and it seemed as if there was nothing on the other side of them, and its tentacles were dripping wet for some time before appearing solid and slimy and all the time ready to crush and kill.

"How has no one discovered this thing, yet?" Kurt found himself asking. It loomed towards the quay on the north bank, claws digging into the walkway that ran over the water. Evidence, at least, that it had been there.

It pulled itself up, writhing and hissing and so clearly unsure how it would survive on dry land. Even Dublin's rainy season wouldn't have been enough for it to last for too long. It needed the water. Kurt took a mental note of its difficulties outside the river.

His head began to ache, and he was suddenly aware of what made this dream different to the others: the Mind's Eye was showing him the whole thing. If he had to guess, he'd assume it was waiting for him to be strong enough, practiced enough, to manage it.

Kurt needed more time. He ignored the headache, focusing now on the magic that flowed from the creature. All monsters had signatures. It was how anyone ever found them. This one was different. It was like it had been sewn together from several pieces, and knotted up in all sorts of charms and spells. Nothing so pure as the protection spells he'd practiced for years. This was different. Darker magic, the sort he refused to get too comfortable with. Darkness taints.

At its core, a binding spell, one that Kurt didn't recognise. It held the water in place, and tied the shape and form of the creature together. Its mind was made from raw instinct.

He didn't need magic to know what its drive was in life. It was looking at a couple of men staggering down the road, animalistic hunger burning in its eyes. "Gods, no," Kurt muttered.

He didn't like to judge, but he could tell immediately what made the men different to anyone else who might have passed the area that night. They were homeless.

Homeless meant different things to different people, but there was always one thing that rough sleepers had in common: people didn't know when they'd go missing or when they'd just move to another area. Not always. And not after just a day or two. If Kurt was right, and he had a sneaking suspicion that he was, everyone else he believed to have been attacked by the monster of the Liffey had been like the two men below.

One was drunk. The other was trying to help him. A tentacle grabbed the sober man before he noticed the lizard-like head peering over the river's edge.

"What the f-"

He was ripped from the ground in an instant, screaming as several more tentacles grabbed onto him in mid-air, lashing for him like whips until they made contact.

Kurt watched the other man run, afraid, blinded by drink and fear. He didn't know what he'd seen. The one witness, and he was unreliable.

His friend let out a roar for help as sharp claws and sharper teeth tore into is flesh. Blood was lapped up by the tentacles. Whole body parts were consumed without the lizard needing to use its mouth. It was digging into the man's chest, the whole thing practically concealed from view. Kurt could still see as the lizard's razor tongue plucked the heart from the man's chest, and swallowed it in one piece.

The world shook, a blast of light disturbing the night sky. Kurt recognised it. The same thing that had given him the worst headache the last two mornings.

"Gotcha," he whispered.

The lizard looked up at him, seeing through the veil of dreams and warped spacetime and the sort of magic that allowed someone to spy on a city while they were supposed to be sleeping. It devoured the rest of the man, every part of its body capable of eating.

Kurt didn't know what it could do to him. Tentacles rose up out of the water in a vaguely threatening manner, surrounding him in every direction, climbing to his altitude.

"I'm no one's midnight snack," he told it.

He woke up in his own bed, panting for breath. That was it, then. That was his case. A great big mess of a monster in a city that he hadn't visited since he was a child. He sat upright, and looked at the time. It was just after two in the morning, and he wasn't sure he'd manage to get some sleep again, not after what he'd witnessed. It wasn't the first time he'd seen someone die, but that didn't make it easier.

He lay there for an hour, unmoving, restless and trying to stop himself feeling anything. He knew where he had to go, just as soon as he figured out what was going on with Edward Armstrong.

Sometimes the job got in the way of the work.

Kurt was ready and waiting for Edward to reappear from his apartment. London was chilly in the morning, as is often the case, but it was dry. Kurt used a small spell to keep himself warm, rather than adding layers to his outfit. Edward had dressed more sensibly.

He avoided the Underground. This became evident to Kurt when his client first approached the station, then immediately turned around. He didn't need to guess why. If someone was following Edward, being trapped in the Tube was a sure fire way to get caught or cornered.

So he kept to the open air, which helped Kurt keep up without imposing. He could monitor Edward's activity as he went into shop after shop, first a bookstore and then a newsagents for a bottle of water, and finally into an old school game shop. He passed time like he had nothing better to do, no job to hide away in, no family to visit, no friends to talk to, and the picture of Edward in Kurt's head began to change.

He wanted so much for the other man to just relax and talk to someone. No one, Kurt reasoned, should be alone.

They stopped at a café. Edward was having lunch, which only served to remind Kurt that he hadn't eaten again. Magic was burning through him, sustaining him, and keeping him on edge, but that sort of behaviour was destined to wear him down in the long run. He ducked into a shop and grabbed a cold sandwich, wolfing it down ungracefully while Edward sipped at a cup of coffee.

Eventually his anxiety hit, the way it had during their meeting, and Edward had to leave.

Kurt followed him to the cinema, where Edward vanished once again. There was no point following him in, so Kurt waited outside. He found a rooftop to sit upon, the height dizzying.

He thought about his last life. He used to sit up on rooftops, watching the sunset over the horizon with the girl of his dreams. They'd sit side by side, looking outward, and when darkness landed over London, they were ready. They fought, always together, against the armies of the night, creatures with fangs and teeth and fur, against the Witches of the Mourning Hour, against vampires and demons and the occasional rogue wizard with a bit of a power up and a head for grandiosity.

They had been the days.

It wasn't always fighting. They went to concerts and went dancing and sometimes just spent lazy Saturdays in oversized clothing reading fiction. They ate breakfast out every now and then, and Kurt would cook them dinner. They would stargaze and they would kiss and they would be together, forever - if forever had an expiry date.

He sighed heavily, and pulled out his phone. It rang, once, twice, and finally - "Hello?"

"Arnold, it's Kurt," he said quietly.

"You got my letter," Arnold cheered. "I have to tell you, that is a relief. I was worried you might have moved after... well..."

Kurt smiled, despite himself. "Still there Arnold. What's been troubling you?"

The thing about Arnold was, he never seemed nervous. He was older than anyone else Kurt liked, and more powerful than anyone else Kurt knew.

But his voice cracked when he spoke. "Something bad, Kurt."

"Something even the most skilled necromancer I know, and the only Reaper I know, can't deal with? I find that hard to believe."

Arnold scoffed at his response. "Are you coming to help?"

Kurt shook his head, forgetting for a moment that he was on the phone. "I have a case. And there's something going on over here. Something only I can fix." He paused, waiting for Arnold to get annoyed at him, to shout, to sigh, to express anything. He was met with silence, a terrible waiting period. "A few days, I think. I just need a few days."

He wasn't sure that he was telling the truth. Odds were, though, that if he didn't stop the creature in Dublin in a few days, he'd never manage it. Greater forces would be called in. City destroying forces.

Arnold seemed satisfied with that. "A few days. Do you want me to call you, or..?"

"I'll call," Kurt insisted. "You have my number now, if you really need to talk sooner, but I have to stay and I don't know…" He trailed off. He didn't want to admit how much out of his depth he was. "I'll call. I promise. I want to see you guys again."

Edward reappeared, stepping out of the cinema pale as a ghost. It had only been just over an hour.

"Damn it, I have to go, Arnold."

"Duty calls?"

"Duty calls, old friend. I'll see you soon."

He fell the distance to the ground, landing gently on the path. Edward hadn't seen him. He was too busy throwing up. Kurt was less concerned with that than he ought to have been. His attention was fixed on a man peeking around the corner. The Mind's Eye flared, and Kurt knew immediately: the man had magic surrounding him, the sort that kept him invisible to most people. The same spells that Kurt used

When Edward moved, so did the man. With no way of getting closer to him without alerting his client, Kurt ran forward. "Mr Armstrong, get back inside," he yelled, charging at the man who he knew to be following Edward.

"What's going on?" Edward screamed.

A fireball burst into life in Kurt's palm. "I found your stalker." The chase began.

The man was easy to keep track of, even without the Mind's Eye screaming at Kurt about him the entire time. He was dressed all in black, clothes almost fit for parkour, but none of the athleticism to match. He stamped along the ground, big boots sounding their presence to the world. He was slight and wiry, a wizard wholly dependant on magic.

But he was fast. Kurt had to give him that. He'd clearly grown up running.

There were too many crowds for either of them to move easily. The runaway ducked down a side alley, one that seemed to materialise out of nothing. Wizards and their tricks, Kurt grumbled internally.

He followed, the path threatening to vanish at any moment. The way behind him shut, and the floor began to shift from concrete to carpet. Bricks slid into place in front of him.

Kurt screamed something in Latin, and the wall exploded out of his way, bricks crashing against the wizard's back. Wary of Damage Control tracking them, Kurt repaired the wall as he ran, a flick of his wrist slamming the bricks back into place.

At least he'd done something. His prey was injured.

That didn't stop him running into traffic. Cars slammed on their brakes for him, though one almost hit Kurt as he hurried in pursuit. London wasn't made for wizards on the run. Kurt couldn't throw a fireball to slow down the man. He couldn't tie his feet up with concrete or summon a blinding light all around him. He couldn't use a telekinetic push to throw him off balance. There were too many people in the way, and too many witnesses who didn't know about magic. Damage Control would have his head several times over if he revealed the truth about the magical community over a simple job.

More alleys opened up for the wizard, but Kurt was closer this time. He wasn't trapped when he reached the other side, and he didn't need to break anything. Which was a pity, he thought. He would have liked to break something.

"Stay away from me," the man screamed back, a thick Scottish accent roaring over the Londoners.

"You stay away from my client!"

The man dug his hand into his pocket, pulling out a handful of sand. He threw it, glowing and almost on fire, straight ahead. A portal ripped open. Kurt was right behind him, so close to catching him, when they fell through the other side. The man continued running with ease.

Kurt was less fortunate. He was thrown out the other side twenty feet in the air, falling instead of running. He barely slowed himself down. The wizard had increased the gap between them when Kurt started running again.

It was all tricks, Kurt thought. The alleys, the portal: they were accessories, not the man's real abilities.

"You're not getting away," Kurt hissed, heart pounding, lungs burning.

But he was. The man ran into a park, right into a grove of trees, and was swallowed by the ground. Kurt followed him, but it took a moment to convince the trees to tell him where the man had gone.

By that point, there was a considerable distance between them, and the man seemed to have recovered from his injuries. He was increasing his gap.

Kurt had no choice. Magic poured into his legs, burning brightly through his trousers, and his pace picked up. He would pay the toll, later. The extended effort allowed him to catch up just as the man smashed his way through the front door of an old house. Kurt was right behind him as he jumped face first onto the sofa and vanished.

"Son of a... okay, first time for everything," Kurt said to himself.

He dove into the sofa, and was sucked through the fabric with a pop; emerging in a parked taxi. The backseat door was open.

"What's going on?" the driver wailed.

"Just business, sir. Forget you ever saw me." The man had lost all colour in his face. "Damn it, I hate doing this," Kurt said to himself. He planted a hand on the man's head. "Forget you saw me," he said forcefully.

The driver went still, dazed for a moment. A smile slowly crept to his face when he heard music from the radio, and his attention slipped away from Kurt entirely. Kurt grimaced as he left the taxi. Though he had a speciality in it, Kurt hated using memory magic on others. It was meant for caring and healing. It was the only thing that kept Kurt sane over the years.

He didn't have time to worry about whether he'd been too rough on the man. The runaway wizard was getting away.

The Mind's Eye lit up a path before him. It was helpful, Kurt had to admit, but worrying. The spell was interfering more and more with his perception of the world. This must have been what Madame Madness had warned him about, he reasoned. Eventually, he would only see as the Eye saw, until it was gone and the world failed to make any more sense.

So he hurried. He ran faster than he thought he could, magic burning in him, and he caught up.

The Thames blocked the way forward. The runaway wizard stood at the water's edge, and looked back at Kurt. His eyes were wide with terror.

"What do you want with Edward Armstrong?" Kurt asked him. Fireballs exploded into life in the palms of his hands. It was a trick he never forgot.

The other man swallowed hard. "You wouldn't risk exposure out here," he whimpered.

The air crackled around them, distractions rippling through space in such volume and velocity that no one would think twice of coming anywhere near them. Car engines would stall. Phones would drop. Someone would crash if need be, causing a traffic jam. A football would break a window. A bird would excrete on someone's head.

"No exposure," Kurt told the man. The effort the spell took was enormous, worse than he'd feared, but he had to hold it up. London was a busy city, these days. "Now answer the question."

The man edged towards the water. "My employers would end me if I spoke about it," the man replied. "Just let us have him. It's better for everyone that he doesn't…" He stopped himself. "You made a mistake interfering, Kurt Crane."

"So you've heard of me."

"Everyone has heard of you," the man replied. He pulled down his hood, revealing a line of stitches from his forehead across the top of his bald head, and magic circles carved into the flesh on each side. "The man who can't stay dead. The man who needs no necromancy. The walking miracle."

"That's a little more than most people know," Kurt acknowledged.

A grin spread across the man's face. "I am but a humble servant, Crane, but know this: my employers are watching you now. You should have stayed out of this."

The man dropped backwards into the river. There was no splash.

Kurt scowled, hurrying to the water's edge. He was gone, and the detective didn't have a clue who he was. The Mind's Eye lit up a symbol in the water, one of the same he'd seen the day before, glowing dimly.

The man was gone.

Kurt found a shortcut through a laundry back to the cinema, with only a mild amount of discomfort as a washing machine swallowed him and he fell out of a tree a block away from where he'd left Edward.

His magical reserves were running low, but he couldn't let Edward know that.

"Jesus, you look like crap," his client told him.

"Thanks for the honesty, I guess," Kurt mumbled. "We need to get you home." Edward looked at him worriedly. "The guy got away. He wasn't acting alone. You've attracted some attention. Something about you is special to these people."

Edward threw up again. "Oh God, they're going to kill me, aren't they?"

"Not if I can help it."

"But they were following me all this time," Edward moaned.

Kurt shook his head. "I was following you yesterday. And this morning. I don't know how long they've been watching you."

Edward sat on the ground, defeated. "You? This whole time?" His eyes were searching the air for answers. "It feels like... like I've been followed by someone for days. Weeks, maybe. My head is a mess, Mister Crane. I don't know when this started, anymore. It's all spinning."

Kurt knelt down in front of him. "Edward, let me take you home. You need to be somewhere safe. I can put up protection spells. I can keep them away until we figure out what they really want."

"But you're part of this," Edward insisted. "You're wrapped up in all of this. I can see it so clearly, now." He paused. "You did something to a taxi driver a few minutes ago."

Kurt swore under his breath. "Yes. A memory spell. I accidentally appeared in the back of his car after a couch swallowed me. I didn't have time for him to freak out or draw attention to me."

Suddenly Edward's demeanour softened. "Well that makes sense, I guess." It didn't, Kurt thought, but at least he didn't need to try explain it any further. "Memory magic. Have you used it on me before?" He didn't wait for a response. "No, you haven't. But you're thinking about it. There's a possibility that you'll use it to try make me make sense of what I've been afraid of. You want to unjumble my head. You want to sort out all the little pieces, and turn me into someone I'm not."

The magician found himself speechless. "Oh, you're very good." He held out a hand, and Edward accepted the help to his feet. "There's a reason I don't use that magic too often. Memories make people who they are. Start changing the memories and you lose the identity of who you're talking to."

They took their time walking. Kurt needed the chance to recover. His legs were aching from exerting himself so much in the chase.

He told Edward about the memory magic on the way. It was entirely academic. Though not illegal, there was a strict licencing program held by Damage Control about the use of memory magic. It required years of study in psychology, neurology, and ethics before practical lessons began, and those were only performed on people whose minds were already fractured enough that they could only really be helped.

Kurt had learned to use the magic long before such research had been done on the human mind. He had helped perfect the skills required.

"But that doesn't mean I get to use it on just anyone," he said quietly. "Dire circumstances, and…"

"Self-treatment," Edward finished. "That's why you studied it, right?" He stopped. They were outside his building. "I know things I shouldn't, Mister Crane. What if that's why they want to kill me?"

"I'll figure it out, Edward, don't you worry," Kurt told him. The effort required to believe himself in his instance was greater than Kurt would ever dare admit to a client. This was a new sort of case. Missing persons or complicated curses or monsters under the bed, all easy. He could deal with them, because he knew what he was up against. And, he had to admit, he usually had a bit of a warm up to the gig before things got messy.

He followed Edward indoors. The building was cramped, the stairway to Edward's flat thin and creaky. There were three locks on Edward's door.

"Are any of these new?" Kurt asked him.

Edward shook his head. "I've always been a bit nervous." He placed his shopping on the kitchen worktop. It was a studio apartment, messy and disorganised. Kurt imagined it might have smelled quite poorly. "Sorry about the state of the place. The past few days have been… well, worse than usual. Have a seat if you can find a place. I'll get the kettle on."

After moving what looked like clean clothes onto the bed, Kurt sat in an armchair. It wasn't comfortable, but it was a relief to get the weight off his legs.

He allowed himself the respite of some healing magic. He could manage just a bit without damaging the muscle fibres in his legs permanently. Body modification magic was a tricky business. Increasing the strength of a muscle could tire it out, and he'd so far had a couple of overly serious workouts since starting the case, after a lifetime of taking it relatively easy. He knew, without needing anyone to say it to him, that he had to be careful.

"Can you give me a few minutes of quiet?" Kurt ask Edward. "I just need to examine the place a bit, and the chase was a bit more draining than I'd have liked." Edward nodded, and Kurt directed his attention back to the room.

The Mind's Eye explored the apartment with vigour. It tried to find a root cause for any changes in Edward, changes that the Eye either couldn't see, or refused to show him out of sheer defiance.

The place was, in magical terms, clean.

Kurt allowed himself to give into the Eye's prodding even further, which was a certain one-way trip down the road of insanity. It looked into Edward, finding a jumbled mess of anxiety, obsessive compulsions, and a hint of magical energy that hid from view.

Almost everyone had it. The potential to learn how to use magic lay in waiting, sometimes activating sporadically, and just the once, and other times never appearing at all. It fed the imagination, and it allowed an athlete to push herself just that little bit further. It let mothers lift cars when their children were in need, and saved people when they were free-falling towards certain injury.

What was inside Edward wasn't enough to allow him to know the things he knew, or to be a target for some unknown group of wizards who carried gadgets over using their own spells. The Mind's Eye closed, returning Kurt back to the apartment in peace.

"I've got nothing," he muttered, and Edward practically slammed two cups of tea down.

"I'm sorry. I know you're just trying to help. But honestly, it feels like I'm drowning under a sea of fire and water, Mr Crane, too hot or too cold and totally incapable of breathing. And…"

He paused, and Kurt stood up. He placed a hand on Edward's shoulder, and decided against using magic to fix the situation. "Your anxiety, Edward. That's all this is." The other man nodded. "Now, let's put this place into safety mode."

Paul Carroll

Chapter Five: Lost and Found

There was no official protocol for protecting a house from intruders, particularly when the intruder possessed an undisclosed proficiency for magic. Kurt had a mental checklist of charms and protective spells that he would normally use, beyond a radial alarm for magical activity.

He had Edward sit down with his tea, hoping that his anxiety would settle after a few minutes of observing the detective dubbed the Magic Man at work.

Kurt had earned the name decades ago, when he displayed magic that hadn't been seen in centuries. He couldn't reveal to people how he had managed to cast the spells, or how he had learned such forbidden magic as angel smiting, and such ancient magic as retrocognition, but the display of such skills had amazed all the right people, and all the wrong future bureaucrats.

He wouldn't need to smite anyone - he hoped - but he could still put his expertise to good use. It wasn't what he expected when he had taken the job.

He started with a protection charms in the door. It would, in theory, prevent unwanted entry. The spell was derived from older warding spells, but modified following an excessive binge of all seven seasons of *Buffy the Vampire Slayer*. Kurt liked the idea of an invite granting entry past an otherwise unbreakable barrier, particularly given the magic used to sustain it was old enough that most wizards couldn't figure out how to unseal it. The protection spell would, in theory, also wrap around to cover the windows, but he didn't want to take any risks.

Pricking his fingers, he inscribed blood seals on the windows. Enochian magic, from the angels themselves, would ward off evil. The glass itself was protected by the spell, and by the barrier.

Stealing some of Edward's salt - further adding to the man's confusion, Kurt poured lines around the door and along the window sills. "Why?" Edward asked sceptically. "The other things I get. They look magical. They sound magical. But this is just salt."

"Not when you know what you're doing with it," Kurt told him. "An experienced hunter or a wizard of some esteem can turn a simple salt line into a barrier against spirits and demons. It'll keep you safe, I promise. We don't know what we're up against."

"How bad could it get?" Edward asked. To Kurt, he seemed worried beyond his usual anxiety. "What sort of magic could you be protecting me against?"

Kurt shook his head. "No way to tell. The guy I chased, he looked stitched together, and he had access to all sorts of spells for creating paths and moulding reality around him, but none of it was his. There's a chance his employers are well equipped with magical artefacts that I know nothing about." He slumped down onto a chair in the kitchen. "This isn't all pointless, I promise. If they come, no matter what sort of magic they use, they won't break through. The power required to breach the seal around your apartment will alert the Powers That Be and Damage Control quicker than it'll take me to get here. One way or another, you're going to be fine."

Edward seemed to relax, but when Kurt stood up, hands glowing, he had to ask. "You're not done?"

"I just have one more little trick to add to the mix," Kurt told him. He grabbed a couple of large bottles of water, filled to the brim, and poured magic through them. "Improvised holy water. Pour it into the kettle, drink plenty of tea. It'll be harmless to you, but it'll renew certain protection spells every time the steam enters the air."

For what seemed like the first time, Edward chuckled. "That's actually a good idea," he said, smiling. "I can do that. I can drink tea like the best of them."

"I'm counting on it, Edward."

He left the apartment to the sound of the kettle boiling, drained and weary, but proud of the work he'd done. He took a few minutes to catch his breath properly, safe from the watching and worried eyes of Edward Armstrong.

The man was a mystery to him. He had made a mental checklist of everything he thought might be wrong with him and with the case, and aside from a few mental health issues, there was nothing much to add.

He didn't seem to demonstrate magical abilities, whether they manifested as psychic powers or not, yet he knew things without needing Kurt to tell him. He'd known about Baker Street, and when to show up, and he had known about Kurt's routine memory fixing as part of a self-care process that had kept him on the relatively sane side of things for longer than he cared to admit.

He wasn't possessed, or he would have known. Either his own magic or the Mind's Eye would have picked up on that. He was exactly who he said he was and who he presented as in public and in private: a relatively nice guy with a crappy apartment, who seemed to be between jobs or taking a break, and whose anxiety was contributing to a case of paranoia.

"Except that he was right," Kurt noted as he left the building. Edward Armstrong had been followed, by Kurt and by the stitched-up man, and he had known.

The Mind's Eye did not like the display of magic around the apartment. It was obvious to it, as a spell that could see through realities, that a lot of work had gone into keeping the building safe. Kurt was sure no one else would notice until they tried to break in.

Still, he spread his alarm radius out further. The effort almost made him throw up. He really needed to rest.

He stumbled into a fast food restaurant, an American place that served portions that were way too big and way too salty and just the right amount of bad for him that he needed. He inhaled a double bacon cheeseburger as quickly as he could, and collapsed into his seat. He still had what probably qualified as three portions of fries in front of him, and a milkshake that would probably kill him, and for the first time in years he felt satisfied with some of his decision making.

Food was important, he admitted. Food helped with recovering magical energy. Food and sleep and taking one's mind of things. These were all pressing concerns that other people had had for him for years, when he still had other people around him. He almost lamented, when he was struck with a thought.

"That's why it eats the way it does," he gasped. He drew a couple of stares, and threw back a glare in response.

The monster in the Liffey flooded his thoughts. It was eating for the energy, and growing bigger for it. He scribbled down the idea. He would need to confirm it at some point, to verify that he wasn't simply delirious or insane.

"But what does it have to do with Edward?" he asked himself. As far as he knew, Edward and the monster were completely unrelated cases. One was a man being followed, the other was a monster with an insatiable appetite.

He needed to think on it. He needed more information. He feared he would get it if he slept, to be woken by the echoing screams of the monster's next meal. It caused him to shudder, and when people rolled their eyes at him, he regretted not putting out some distractions. But he was worn out from his earlier work at the Thames. There was only so much he could do, even when he wasn't still getting used to his power again, and he didn't think judgemental diners were anything to be threatened by.

He had more pressing concerns, like figuring out why someone would want Edward dead, and gathering some supplies to reinforce the shield at his apartment in case something happened to Kurt to weaken the spell retrospectively.

Stranger things had happened.

Peter Hughes sat in front of his television, filled with nonsense nerves. The Lotto was on, the numbers being displayed one by one exactly as he had predicted. He bit his nails, one by one until they were all gone, and resorted to hyperventilating until they finished.

"Six grand," he whispered. "What the hell am I supposed to do with six grand?"

He started pacing the room. He had done it. He'd cheated, and he'd won and now he was a few thousand euro richer. He knew Damage Control wouldn't suspect a thing. He knew no one would try to exploit him. He had his money, and he had his power to see into the future infallibly, and he was freaking out as if he had just stabbed someone in the chest repeatedly and now had a body to get rid of.

"Who do I call?" he whispered. "Jesus, what will Mammy say? What will the neighbours think?" He racked his brain, and memories of his foretelling trickled back into his head. "Christ, I'm supposed to go for drinks with everyone to celebrate. I don't want to do that. What if someone finds out I'm a bloody psychic? What if by knowing that no one will find out, I accidentally reveal it?"

He sank into his couch. Being psychic was less fun than he ever thought it might be.

He poured himself a drink, gin and tonic, and was halfway towards drinking it when he put the glass down. He needed sobriety. The only thing worse than a psychic having anxiety was a drunk psychic having anxiety.

"What do I do?" he whimpered.

He looked into the future, and it was changed. There was no party, because no one knew he'd won.

No, that wasn't right. Everyone was out for drinks without him. He didn't show up. He couldn't show up. He didn't know why. Peter couldn't make himself look for a reason why he would miss a night out that, no matter how much he didn't want to go, he didn't want to miss. Something inside him wouldn't let him look for an answer.

But that didn't matter anymore, because now there was another problem. Now he knew the future wasn't fixed. He could predict something, but that didn't mean it was definitely going to happen. Knowing the outcome of the lottery had only guaranteed him the prize, not the celebrations. As soon as a choice was made, everything else shifted.

"What about Missus Gillespie?" he found himself asking. "What if I should have just let her die?"

He didn't like that thought, and before he could stop himself he down the gin and tonic. The alcohol seemed to rush to his head, like the power to change the future. He had broken something fundamental in the universe. He had changed someone's death date, and he didn't know if it was possible to put it back.

Would he have to kill Missus Gillespie? Was there a time travelling cop from the future on his way to Dublin to remove her from the timeline? And what about him? Was he going to be punished for accidentally saving someone's life when he didn't even know that what he'd seen was real?

It was all too much. He poured another drink. He forgot to add the ice. He wished he had a cucumber to add to the gin. He downed the glass. His head spun. He tried to look into the future again.

Everything hit him at once. Glasses clinking in a pub. His mother crying. Missus Gillespie watching every car every time she tried to cross the road. People screaming. Lots of them. Peter included. A ragged man in a flannel shirt throwing fireballs.

Another drink.

Another look into the future. Teeth. Someone hit by a car, the same car. And box in the boot of a moving cat, a cat in the box with a bottle of gin filled up with toxic green poison, and no way of knowing when it would break.

Nothing made sense and everything was happening too quickly and all at the same time, even the things that could only happen if something else didn't.

He stopped himself before another drink, afraid he'd only look into the future again. What if he got careless? What if he aimed bigger, next time? What if he kept changing the little things in the future, until it all spun out of control? There had to be rules for this sort of power. He knew there had to be. He could see a future where he discovered the rules and he stuck to them out of fear and morality and because he was convinced that you could change one thing because it was the right thing to do and because the universe needed it to happen.

But he didn't know, now, what those things were. What was more important, Peter being able to afford his rent - and therefore help more people - or Missus Gillespie avoiding an accident? Did there have to be balance? Did he have to choose between personal gain and the wellbeing of others? Was every life as important as the next?

He had another drink. He wished he hadn't.

Peter passed out on his couch.

Kurt didn't own maps. He didn't own a lot of things. He summoned a map of Dublin from a charity shop, and promised himself he'd pay them another time. It was out of date, anyway.

He pinned it to his wall, and stuck more pins in where he knew the monster had struck. A clear section of the river was blocked out, between two bridges, and including a third in the middle.

"Millennium, Ha'penny, O'Connell. Why there?"

He hadn't been to Dublin in a long time, but he guessed it had to do with the foot traffic. Lots of people to observe. Lots of people to feed upon. And with the darkness of the water, and the way the monster could blend in with it, lots of space to hide. Three bridges to hide under.

The media was missing something. Only now were people noticing the missing homeless men. Kurt didn't know how many. Five or six so far, and one survivor.

He'd spoken to a charity worker. He couldn't find his friend, his only friend in the world. They were trying to find somewhere to sleep. He was drunk. And they were separated.

'What if he's dead?' was the quote they were throwing around online.

There was no doubt about it, Kurt knew. He was dead, and a few others like him and gone before him, and no one knew who they were. No one knew the men who had gone missing, or how to figure out where they could have gone if they weren't dead.

"They're all blind," Kurt muttered, and he wasn't sure if he was angry at them or at the fact that he couldn't help yet. Not until Edward was safe.

They weren't talking about checking the river yet, which bought Kurt a little bit of time. He had a sick feeling in his stomach that if they checked the river they'd stir the monster. He didn't want to consider the casualties.

He sank into his chair. He didn't have contacts in Dublin who cared to talk to him, but he put a call in with an old friend who ran a supply store in Belfast. He hadn't heard of any attacks in Dublin. No one was talking about it. No one was covering it up.

Which meant, Kurt could finally confirm, no one was trying to stop it. Damage Control were oblivious. The magical community didn't know if they should be on the lookout for anything that might risk exposure. Kurt didn't know how to raise a red flag about these things, not without a small army descending on him.

He'd had another reason for calling the store, anyway, aside from fishing for gossip and rumours. He needed some physical charms, magical objects, to give to Edward. He couldn't quite give all the details to his supplier, but the general idea was enough.

Damage Control were reasonable about magical purchases. So long as something couldn't be used for malevolent purposes, there were no restrictions in place, and any use of teleportation magic for them wasn't tracked. It didn't matter to them who felt the need to protect themselves; everyone worried about something, whether it was a magical threat or household robbers.

A paper bag popped into existence at the street corner near Kurt's apartment a few minutes later, where the magic man stood in waiting with a distraction field up around him. He couldn't risk giving away his actual address, even to a trusted supplier, and everyone who would still talk to Kurt understood that. Discretion was key to staying out of trouble. The less anyone knew, Kurt reasoned, the better. Even Damage Control, with their best intentions, could lose a run of themselves sometimes.

As well as some of the usual supplies one would need to sustain protection spells, Kurt had ordered a new book on symbology. His old ones were likely divided between the mess in his apartment and the mess in his office, and he didn't fancy tackling either one.

He took another look at the Dublin case. It was too late to go back to Edward's apartment. With a bit of luck, the man had fallen asleep.

He had no hopes for identifying the monster in the Liffey. He'd sketched it, something he was proud of as a normal, human sort of magic, and was still drawing a blank. He thought he'd seen everything already. There was nothing like it in the books, nothing like it in his past, and nothing like it in folklore. It was a new monster, and a nasty one.

New monsters were a rare problem, but a major one. People weren't especially good at predicting their behaviour, and he had a feeling that he would struggle against this one in a fight if he was trying not to destroy Dublin in the process. There were no recorded fights with this sort of monster. He didn't know if ice magic would slow it down, if fire would hurt it, if electricity would conduct - or whether there was anyone else in the water - or whether the creature could be transmuted into something more breakable.

That was only half the problem. It was getting bigger. He knew intuitively that the next time it struck, it would be bigger still. Bigger from eating, taking up more of the Liffey, getting more dangerous to people all around it.

At some point it would stop sleeping. He had no doubt about that. It would come alive during daylight hours, and it would feast on the thousands of people who passed by its three-bridge hunting grounds.

"I'm running out of time and out of ideas," he said to himself. "And I still have the bloody symbols in the Thames to think about. There has to be a connection to Edward's case."

The new book was thick, full, and useless. It told him, in not so many words, that the symbol didn't exist. It, too, was new. The only things he could find that were remotely close to it were symbols of water magic. While that made sense to

Kurt, it was still about as useful as a sketch of the unknown monster and a last known sighting of the stitched up man.

"Gods damn modern magicians and their complete reliance on technology. Damn their information networks, damn their refusal to commit things to books that people like me can buy, borrow or steal, and damn them for being so bloody unobservant when the world is breaking around them." He scowled at the book of symbols, totally useless to him. "They missed a giant water monster in Dublin, a river full of magical symbols in the Thames, and a massive display of magical energy in London."

He tossed the book away. He always felt guilty abusing books in this manner, but he felt this one deserved it. *The Greater Encyclopedia and Reference Guide to Symbols Old & New for the Budding Magician, Twenty-Fifth Edition* had proved itself a complete waste of paper, ink and effort, and if Kurt ever found the person responsible for throwing it together, he'd likely have to punch them in the face.

There was nothing on the symbols in the Thames, nothing on the symbols etched on the stitched man's head, and nothing on what to do when the book was so bloody useless that budding magicians would die in an instant if they relied on it. He wanted to burn the book, but thought better of it.

There would be a better time for fireworks and toxic displays of wizardry. Now was a time for sleep, and the great expectation of being stirred from whatever he called slumber. Now was the time the beast would awake.

Paul Carroll

Chapter Six: Screams in the Night

There was an attack at two in the morning, and Kurt slept through it. That is to say, the Mind's Eye didn't force him to bear witness. He supposed that the last time had been too close for comfort. The monster had seen him, as impossible as that sounded to Kurt. So he slept, right up until the kill, but he felt it all.

It was more daring, now. The creature moved with distinct ideas in its head about who to attack and when, and how to get away with it. Kurt could feel intention burning in his brain, a force so strong that it could override a wizard's need for rituals and special words. The monster possessed intention like nothing Kurt had ever witnessed in any living being. It knew exactly the outcome it wanted, and it struck without hesitation.

The screams woke Kurt. Fear, pain, and youth. Three of the worst things Kurt could imagine being combined into one sound.

The news would announce their deaths in the morning, when one of their handbags would be found splattered in blood. Samantha Donovan and Jessica Cummins. College students, a little bit drunk at their time of death, but innocent.

Kurt could feel their identities, see their faces, anguish at their suffering, all from his bed. He had sweated through the t-shirt he'd fallen asleep in, and ripped his bedsheets apart with a burst of magical energy. Anything to relieve the tension. He hadn't done that in lifetimes.

That wasn't the worst of it. The Mind's Eye lit up the apartment in a cold green light. It made the mess easier to see. Water from the Liffey covered the floor, lakes of river water around soggy carpet that squelched when stood upon.

The map of Dublin was slashed in two. The weak glow of a tentacle on his desk caught his attention. A piece of the monster, fading away as he watched it.

"What the bloody hell is going on?" Kurt muttered, as his phone began to ring.

Peter Hughes' throat was sore from screaming when he woke up. Before he gave himself a chance to think about what he had witnessed, he ran to the toilet. He gagged, thinking he might throw up, but nothing came. He stayed on his bathroom floor.

Two girls had been killed and he'd watched it happen. It didn't feel he'd seen the future. It was more like staring helplessly while innocent animals were slaughtered. Animals in high heels, dolled up and half drunk and full of joy. College students, he knew, and it felt like he knew everything about them.

Samantha Donovan was just starting a new relationship. Her boyfriend was from Cork. It was exciting and new and he was practically foreign. He was at home for some of the summer, and came up to visit whenever he could. He drove. He surfed. He read. And he called her all the time.

Jessica Cummins was getting ready to sell the comic book she'd been illustrating for a year between classes and studying and forced socialisation. She had a big convention to launch the book at. Her girlfriend was incredibly supportive, but also a little under the weather.

They were on a girls night out, Samantha and Jessica, best friends since they were eight. They didn't know about magic or monsters or what to do when one attacked you.

They died screaming each others' names.

Peter finally knew the truth. There were worse things than Damage Control. There was a monster in the Liffey, and he didn't know how to stop it.

He looked into the future, to try find help. There had to be help somewhere. Dublin couldn't survive like this.

He saw himself in the Ilac library. There was a book on the bottom shelf that he swore wasn't there before. A black book, thick and heavy with the thinnest paper imaginable. A phone book. *The Black Pages*. He opened it; he knew exactly what he was looking for, who he was looking for. A man. The Magic Man.

In his bathroom he dialled a number. It was answered immediately.

"Do you have any idea what time it is?" said the voice on the other end of the line.

"I need your help, Kurt Crane," Peter said quickly. "We haven't met yet, but I think we're supposed to. My name is Peter Hughes. I'm a legitimate psychic from Dublin, and there's a monster in the Liffey."

There was silence on the other end of the line for a minute. "That's one heck of an opening," Kurt responded. "How many people know?"

"Alive ones?" He almost answered 'just me', but the truth sprang from his mouth out of instinct. "Half a dozen. Me, a homeless man, a charity worker, a… a vampire working as a psychiatrist, a troll that used to live under O'Connell Bridge, and you. Jesus, a vampire and a troll. Didn't think I'd hear myself say that."

"Peter, concentrate."

"Right, sorry. I'm new to this." He anticipated the next question. "A few days. I've had the power to see into the future for a few days."

"It ties in with the first attack," Kurt said quietly down the phone. "Something weird is happening, Peter."

That went without saying. There were a lot of weird things happening, and Peter couldn't let himself get dragged down the rabbit hole kicking and screaming while answers flooded his head. He had to ignore the idea of something being wrong in London, ignore the vampire and the troll and the fact that there was going to be an accident that he couldn't stop.

"Dublin needs your help, Kurt," Peter said clearly. "I know you have other work, but this is getting bad."

"I've got another case," Kurt replied. "But I'll see what I can do. I've been trying to monitor the situation from here." Peter felt a lie in his words, but he didn't want to call him out on it. "I'll be over as soon as I can. I trust I can contact you on this number?"

"Yes, sir, thank you."

"Don't thank me yet," Kurt said, and hung up the line.

Peter sank against his bathroom door. Relief washed over him. He had done something useful. He had helped.

"Oh Christ," he gasped. "I think I just gave him a death sentence."

Kurt showered and ate - somehow - and waited for a reasonable hour to try call Edward. Six in the morning was about as close as he could get. He booked flights to Dublin from Heathrow at the last minute, a fake passport in his bag with a fake identity, the only way Damage Control couldn't find him. He'd paid heavily for it. Real money, real fake passport, no magic involved.

His phone rang through several times. Edward just wasn't picking up.

"Come on Edward," he muttered.

He went to voicemail for the fifth time, and hung up. There was no sense in leaving a message. He cleaned up his bedroom, struggling to get rid of the river water and incapable of telling how much it smelled. The Mind's Eye was at least sparing him the sensation this early in the morning.

He tried Edward again. Nothing. "Fine. You won't answer your phone? I've still got enough time to knock down your door before my flight."

He left his apartment in a huff, a collection of protection charms inside his impossible bag, along with a few days' worth of clothes, his notebook, pen, crystal ball, and anything else he could find in his apartment that might be useful. He didn't have the time to swing by his office, nor did he have the energy. His legs were heavy walking down the stairs. He was still recovering from the chase and the would-be fight.

He would be damned, though, if he didn't check up on Edward before leaving the country.

Edward missed his phone calls because he had dropped his phone in the cinema. He was awoken early by screaming birds, and had found it impossible to get back to sleep. He was tired from the night before. While drinking an excessive amount of tea, he began to sort through all of the ideas in his head. He began to understand what was happening to him. His memories unfolded and sorted themselves, and sometimes he knew there were fantasies mixed in, but he kept those in when he wrote everything down. He addressed it all to Kurt. The detective needed to know what was going on, and he didn't trust himself to tell it all to someone out loud.

By morning, everything was a bit of a mess again, and he just wanted his phone. He just wanted to connect with the world. To read the news. To avoid messaging his family.

He sighed heavily. He would need to get Kurt to retrieve it for him, since he wasn't allowed to leave the building. He didn't like to think of Kurt as a messenger boy, but the magician had effectively put him on house arrest. It was stay and live, or leave and die, and he knew which one was preferable.

That didn't stop him heading downstairs to retrieve his post. He figured he would be safe doing that. His anxiety had abated considerably since Kurt had put so many protection spells around the place. He just needed to remember to fix the salt line at the door before he got too comfortable again. He had tried to be careful, but there was only so much one could do.

"Oh, a handwritten one," Edward remarked as he walked up the stairs again. The rest were bills, or political memos, or Chinese menus. He dropped them onto the kitchen counter when he reached his flat, forgetting about the salt line, and entirely missing the counter, scattering envelopes across the floor.

He did not recognise the handwriting on the one envelope left in his hands. It was cursive in red ink, beautiful and ornate and far too fancy for anyone he knew to have written it.

He tore it open gently. He thought, for a moment, that it might be a love letter.

But the paper inside had no words on it. It contained only a circle, an eight-sided star, and a series of scribbled-on symbols that he didn't know all the way around the edge of the circle, all handwritten in red ink.

The image glowed from the page, a light-form copy of the circle and its scribbles and its star rising from the page. It pressed against Edward, and his fingers let go of the paper.

It floated before him, while his feet lifted from the ground. His weight was sustained by the magic circle that clung to him, holding him up.

"Oh no," Edward said to himself, recognition flashing across his face. "I'm so sorry Kurt. You probably think you failed…"

The circle exploded into flames, consuming Edward in seconds. Head to toe were burning, and he couldn't scream. His throat wouldn't work. The ceiling was scorched, but the rest of the flat was fine. Held off the floor the way he was, nothing else was touched.

It didn't last long. It didn't need to.

Kurt's alarms were blaring in his head, all of them at once, and he knew something was wrong with Edward. He reached the apartment, the building door locked. He didn't have time to be careful. He grabbed the handle, and applied strength that wasn't his own, breaking the lock loose.

He took the stairs two at a time, almost knocking down a neighbour in his hurry. He didn't apologise. The alarms were still sounding in his head.

Edward's door was closed. Kurt kicked at it with a booted foot, and the whole thing burst into the room, locks and hinges breaking from the doorframe.

There was no smoke, but Kurt could see the smouldering remains of Edward Armstrong on the floor of his kitchen. "Burned alive," Kurt said quietly. "Jesus. Poor guy."

His alarms quietened with him there, but something had to have set them off. The windows were shut, and the salt lines undisturbed except for the one along the door; that had scattered everywhere when the door exploded inwards. There was still a flicker of magic from the water in the kettle, and the perimeter hadn't been breached.

Still, somehow, something had gotten in.

The Mind's Eye did his searching for him, without his command or consent. It was a concern he would have to overlook for the time being. He needed the assistance.

A piece of paper on the floor caught his attention. He picked it up warily, magic clinging to the air around it. "That doesn't look like any magic circle I've ever seen," he noted, spying the handiwork on the page. The ink was black and bold and disconcerting. There was no magic in it, not anymore.

He found the corresponding envelope on the floor, beside unopened bills. The address was handwritten, postage had been paid, and it had gone through the usual systems. No one needed to have gone near Edward for the spell to be delivered, a spell that had gotten past every defence Kurt had put in place.

He wasn't aware of uses of magic like this. But then, wizards didn't usually fall for tricks. Wizards could sense the magic, usually as obstacles to overcome when breaking in somewhere they didn't belong. He thought about the days he'd spent dodging traps in castles that no longer existed, flickers of memories that felt more like fairy tales than hidden histories.

And he thought about how he had let Edward down. Despite his best efforts, despite his barriers and his charms and his warning systems, he'd still forgotten about the possibility of a post bomb. He reasoned it was because few people ever really wrote to him, recent letters aside, but that sort of logic wasn't going to bring Edward back.

He had failed, and he didn't have a chance to do anything about it. The clock was ticking.

He pulled out his phone, and called Arnold. The necromancer was still awake, despite the time difference. "Ready to join us?" Arnold asked, without so much as a hello.

"Not yet," Kurt told him. "Listen, is Gary there? I don't have his number." He could feel Arnold's annoyance through the phone. "It's urgent, Arn. I need him to contact Damage Control for me."

The necromancer sighed heavily into the phone, his tone full of drama. "I do hope you haven't gotten yourself into trouble again, Kurt. There are only so many times Gary can cover for you before someone figures something is up."

"There's been a murder, Arnold. My client is dead. It was magical in nature. I need it checked out by professionals. And covered up. There are charms and symbols all over the place because of me."

"They can probably track you from your blood, Kurt," Arnold warned. "For a little while, anyway. You know how crafty they've gotten."

Kurt nodded, and smiled lightly to himself. Arnold was old, over a hundred, and somehow had developed into both the emotionally open sort of man that people liked these days while remaining a condescending old-timer. Maybe it had to do with his resetting age, Kurt thought, but Arnold always treated him like the younger man.

"I'm on my way to Dublin in a little while, to deal with a crisis situation. If they find me, when they find me, they're going to have a bigger mess to cover up than a man who keeps not dying properly."

Arnold chuckled at that. He liked to see Damage Control out of their depth every now and then, and whether it was hunting him or hunting Kurt or landing right in the middle of a mess they were dealing with, they always managed to entertain him. Kurt remembered how they used to exchange stories about it, two uncatchable men out to save the world and piss of bureaucrats.

"I'll pass your message into Gary when he wakes up," Arnold told him. "We're taking shifts sleeping, but he'll be up soon."

"It's a real mess over there, isn't it Arn?"

Arnold was quiet for a moment. "I'll let you worry about when you get here. Just, go save the world. I'll have Gary give you a call if they find anything unusual. And Kurt, take care of yourself out there. Even this far away we're starting to get real bad vibes."

The line disconnected.

"Thanks Arnold," Kurt muttered softly, and left Edward's smouldering body for the professionals to discover. He took down his barrier and his alarm and headed for the airport.

Chapter Seven: Unfair City

Dublin City was very much like London in many ways, from the language and the sort of nonsense approach to how anyone is supposed to find anything, and the way people behaved as they went about their own business. There was always a feeling that the path of least resistance was through other people, like it would be easier to reach a bus in time if one just shoved everyone else out of the way with their shoulder or a handbag or a pram with a screaming three-year-old inside it.

In other ways, it was quieter, and it was those things that Kurt was suddenly appreciating. There were fewer magicians causing a mess of things in Dublin, presumably because there was no way of really hiding anything. The rest of the magical community in London, insomuch as it could ever be called a community, made it increasingly difficult to get anything done, simply by existing and trying to better their usage of magic.

Everything was monitored, especially with the Damage Control headquarters positioned where it was. Things had been easier when Kurt was younger and London was all his, because superstition kept people from exposing themselves in even the smallest of ways. Few people with magic in the last few centuries really explored their own capabilities. There were, Kurt thought, a lot of potentially powerful witches and wizards who had died before realising what they could do, all because of fear. And it had kept the bloody peace.

Kurt could almost get used to the quiet.

Except, of course, that it had taken a short and uncomfortably flight to get to Dublin, and that was just the beginning of the problems he had with travelling anywhere. He didn't like flying. It wasn't so much the complete suspension of a giant piece of metal that put him off so much as it was the absence of certain types of magic. Energy reacted differently in the air than it did when a wizard had his feet firmly planted on the ground.

Some of it had to do with the shape of the plane, of course, and the natural laws of physics that even magic was sometimes known to obey. There were benefits to it, of course, though Kurt didn't like to even consider them. Tracking spells, for instance, were disrupted by planes. The ungrounding of the spell and the dispersion of magic around the shell of the plane made it impossible to follow someone in the air without some power and experience, and most people lacked the knowhow. The other issue was that everyone knew that tracking spells were disrupted by planes, which made them useless for hiding unless one could stay in the air for much longer than they'd ever like.

The spell that had been inevitably cast to find Kurt would eventually catch up. He knew there was only a matter of time before Damage Control found him. Leaving blood in Edward's apartment had been a bad idea, but he had had no choice.

The other major issue with travelling to another city, not limited to Dublin, was that Kurt didn't know the shortcuts to get around the way he knew them in London. He wasn't sure if there was an easy way to travel from the airport to the city centre, without having to suffer the presence of other people, or where to begin looking for it.

There was a shortcut, of course. Every airport was equipped was exits for the magical community, even if they'd had to be smashed into place with dodgy magic. There were stories, rumours beaten down over the years, of wizards arriving in Dublin and using the shortcut to the city centre, only to end up in Cork by accident. For some people who were used to travelling long distances to get anywhere, this wasn't so big a deal. For anyone with any sort of sense of the value of time and knowledge of the correct workings of portals and interdimensional shortcuts, this sort of mess was not to be tolerated. There was a reason Cork wizards hated Dublin, after all.

Kurt had not ended up in Cork, of course. He had taken an expensive bus full of other people to the city centre, hating every last one of them for the noise they generated and their complete disregard for the relative sanity of anyone else onboard. There were times when Kurt had had to stop himself using magic to seal people's lips, and times when he was sure he was going to pass out as a result of someone else's inane conversation. He had, just the once on the trip, shorted out someone's phone, so they would have to stop talking about how poor their flight had been, and all of the things they were planning on doing in day that would take at least a week.

In normal circumstances, all of this would have been a pain to suffer through. On this trip, the bus journey and the flight had served as brief and poor distractions from the grim and terrible closing of his official case. He wasn't so concerned about the money, though he would have liked to have been paid - if only Edward hadn't been brutally murdered. It was the aftermath he was struggling with, and the fact that it never really felt like it had ended.

Added to the twisting pain in his stomach that he could only assume was guilt was a headache that had thrown him off balance several times since he'd left London. The Mind's Eye was acting up, forcing involuntary glimpses into other realities into his mind, and unveiling secret and old spells woven into the bricks of Dublin city. He saw a man who was most certainly a werewolf, and a woman who might be part god, and he was sure that if either of them were aware of their other-than-human status, neither of them wanted anybody else to know.

He did not enjoy spying on people or accidentally discovering their secrets, nor did he fancy the reason why he was suddenly and randomly losing control of the Mind's Eye. Part of it, he guessed, he could blame on the plane. But the more worrying reality was making itself known to him: he was running out of time with the Mind's Eye, and he hadn't figured everything out yet.

He was facing a permanent alteration in perception, and he wanted to swear blindly about it.

Some things were easier than others, of course. Less than ten minutes after arriving in the city, Kurt found one more thing to bother him about Dublin. Just around the corner from the attacks, as Kurt rounded a corner away from the tramline and heading towards the river, from Abbey Street onto Liffey Street, he was hit by a car.

The driver hadn't been paying attention for a couple of days.

When Kurt Crane came to, he was almost surprised to find that he didn't feel like he had died. Whatever way the car had hit him, and whatever sort of instinct he'd developed over the years of dying savagely, his body had been both protected and healed. This came as something of a relief, though he was still mildly annoyed to find the elbow of his jacket scuffed.

There were people standing around him in a circle, gaping at him like a monkey in a zoo. A man had his hand under Kurt's head. "I really should have seen that one coming," the man said. "I'm Peter, from the phone."

"Peter from the phone," Kurt repeated. "Did I just get hit by a car?"

Peter nodded. "I think he's the same person who almost killed Missus Gillespie the other day, until I warned her."

Everything fell back into place for Kurt. "The man who sees the future," he muttered. "Well, your little act of charity ruined my favourite jacket." It was not Kurt's favourite jacket. His favourite was an old duster jacket that felt too heavy to wear during the summer, but had all the sorts of protection spells and wards that a man with his habit for accidentally getting into fights with world-ending monsters needed. "Rule number one of telling the future: weigh up the consequences before you open your bloody mouth."

He glared at the people all around them, and Peter followed his gaze. "He's alright folks," Peter told them. "Yiz can all feck off, now. Back to your shopping or whatever else you do with yourselves."

The crowd dispersed with a grumble, and Kurt almost forgave Peter for having him run over by a car.

"My hotel check-in isn't until this evening," Kurt said to Peter. He struggled to his feet, still dizzy from the accident. "You can buy me a cup of tea to make up for the displeasure of being a replacement victim in a hit and run."

Peter stared back at him in shock. "You're actually going to blame me for that?"

"Tea," Kurt said firmly, "Or I leave you to fix the mess in this city." He didn't mean it, and he wouldn't have wasted the trip over if he was going to follow through on such threats, but he had the feeling that Peter needed some convincing. "You need to learn to take some responsibility for the futures you try to avert, Peter, or you're going to start getting people killed."

The fortune teller looked away bashfully. "I know," he said quietly. "I didn't know this was going to happen. I just wanted to save Missus Gillespie. It was my first time."

He began leading the way to a nearby coffee shop, dragging his feet. It was a pity plea, Kurt knew, and he couldn't help but fall for it. "When I was younger, I thought burning a CD meant using fire. I made a fireball and practically melted the whole bloody computer. Haven't touched the things, since, except when I had to." Peter ordered their drinks, still quiet and hanging his head, and Kurt had to wait until they were tucked away in the corner before he could continue. "Mistakes happen, is all I'm saying."

"So you're not mad?"

Kurt shrugged. "Still a little pissed off, yeah, but you would be too if someone just ran you over. Or dead. Probably dead." He sipped the tea, still too hot to drink. "But I'm over it. Tell me about why I'm here while I try to let this tea make up for the flight over."

Peter cracked a smile at that, which helped ease the tension. Kurt's capacity to make a car accident seem like the end of world was unmatched, particularly when there was a monster in the Liffey that might *actually* end the world if given the opportunity.

"Well, like I said on the phone, I can see the future. It started a couple of days ago, when I saw Missus Gillespie getting hit by that car, and I stopped it happening. Then I won…" He stopped himself, and looked up at Kurt guiltily. He whispered, "I won a few grand in the Lotto by looking into the future."

Kurt shrugged. "I once tricked a bank owner that the stone I'd made look like gold was the genuine article. They were simpler times. No judgement from me. Just, you know, try not make a habit out of it. You know why?"

"Because Damage Control will lock me up?"

Kurt almost spat out his tea. "Gods, no. Well, maybe, but that's not where I was taking this. Consequences. You need to think about the consequences of everything you find out in the future. Whatever you act on, you've got to be sure that it's either the right thing to do or it's not going to hurt someone by doing it anyway."

He laid down his tea. It was burning his mouth too much. Peter looked at him shyly. "Personal experience?"

The magician almost laughed. "Everything is personal when you live to be my age," he said. "I don't really know that, anymore. My age, I mean. I've lost track."

"Well, what year were you born? That usually helps," Peter joked. His face dropped when a flicker of the future passed through his mind.

Kurt beat him to the punch. "This time around? November 1988. Feels like only a short time ago. Last time... Jesus, I used to be so much better at remembering this stuff. I keep it all in a diary, somewhere." He drank casually from his tea, while Peter gaped. "I know what you're thinking, because I'm thinking about saying it, so one version of me will say it in the future. Yes, I will confirm that you're not going crazy. I've lived and died more times than you would care to think of. I've been to every continent on the planet, studied magic under teachers while the art and science of it was still young, and managed to avoid eternal damnation so far."

"You're like, a god or something," Peter said in awe, his eyes wide and staring. If it weren't for a few casual distractions thrown into the air, Kurt was sure people would be looking at them now. "An actual, real life god."

The detective shook his head, and clicked his fingers. Peter snapped out of it, no magic required. "I'm not a god. I'm a magician. I'm a detective. Some people call me the Magic Man, like it's some sort of title to be proud of. Some people think I'm worth revering, and smart people know to avoid me if at all possible. I'm incredibly useful, and incredibly powerful, and sometimes incredibly smart, but I'm not a god. I age, I tire, and I die, the same as anyone else, and then I come back. Which I suppose is a little bit different."

"A little bit is right," Peter scoffed. He was enjoying the conversation more than Kurt was comfortable with.

"Gods are worshipped. They draw their power from prayer and worship and the sacrifices of others. So don't think of me like that. I don't need other people for me to do the things I do. Usually the opposite." He fell silent for a moment. "What's the city like? With all this going on, I mean?"

Peter filled him in on the most important detail first: ignorance. People knew the girls were missing. They didn't know what had happened to them, though Peter had seen it while sleeping. Kurt decided not to tell him what had happened while he'd slept and the creature attacked. It was unimportant. What mattered now was the city. The papers were reporting missing people, now, but no one had any clue what was really going on.

"Did you get any notion that the magical community was active?" Kurt asked.

"There isn't one, as far as I'm concerned," Peter told him. "I'm alone, here, and I looked into the future: no one will do anything in Dublin to reveal themselves. Either they don't think that they're strong enough to fight this thing, or they aren't brave enough."

Brave and stupid were two interchangeable words that most people were not aware were connected. Kurt had enough experience to know that, maybe, the magical community in Dublin were just smart enough to keep their heads down against something they didn't have any idea about. Knowledge was an issue. There were too many gaps.

"Anyway, I don't plan on staying here for long," Peter added. "I can't stay, not with that thing here."

Kurt let that slide for the time being. He would need Peter, he thought. He was useful. For now, the case demanded details. Kurt pulled out his notebook and pen and started jotting down names. There were already half a dozen missing men and women, when the two college students were included. Peter was able to tell him all of their names, and even where they used to beg.

"No one will talk about it, but everyone knows they're missing. They all have spots in the city. I used to pass a couple of them when I was going for lunch." His own tea was untouched. Kurt urged him, silently, to drink up. There was a special sort of magic in hot tea that people didn't understand. "Anyway, when the girls were attacked, I put the rest together in my head. Social media's been active in identifying the men."

Peter showed him the photos of the victims that were circulating. The girls were presumed dead. Someone had realised the cases were all connected. "There was a man who got away," Kurt remembered. "Is it because of him that the media knows so much?"

The fortune teller nodded, flicking through tabs on his phone. "Drunk when he was found crying about his friend, but he stuck to his story the whole time. He said something grabbed his friend. They think it's a metaphor or something. The poor man's been on the streets for half his life. He doesn't think about metaphors, he thinks about getting through each day. He thinks about where to get another drink and a bite to eat and somewhere to sleep."

He showed Kurt a photo. It was the same tired, drunk man that he'd seen. The same one who got away while the monster turned its attention on Kurt, seeing him through a veil of magic that he hadn't cast himself.

"There's enough of a pattern for people to be worried," Peter said, placing his phone face down on the table so he wouldn't have to look at the victims anymore. "I've tried to see what will happen tonight, but I just keep getting flashes of things that don't have anything to do with the monster.

Like someone buying a burger, or a… God, a vampire biting someone's neck." He looked at Kurt pleadingly. "Are there really vampires? And in Dublin?"

"There are vampires everywhere," Kurt told him. "They hide more, now. The nests are gone. As far as I know, they split up to protect themselves. They get rowdy as a pack. Animalistic. They would've drawn someone's attention by now." He could tell that he hadn't calmed Peter's nerves at all. "They don't kill when they bite. They don't change everyone. They eat small amounts, fairly regularly, so they don't have to."

"Unlike the monster in the Liffey, which eats people entirely," Peter moaned.

A woman glanced in their direction, and Kurt forced out further distractions into the air. "Keep your voice down about that," Kurt told his companion. "I'm keeping the attention away from us, but there's only so much of a filter I can put up."

Peter nodded slowly. "Just a bit panicked," he said quietly.

Kurt reached into his bag. He had more than enough protection charms that had been meant for Edward. He handed one across the table to Peter. "Take this," he insisted. "It won't stop the thing in the Liffey getting you, but it'll keep you safe otherwise. And maybe you'll realise there's some good to the magical world, after all. It's not all death and monsters."

With that, he stood up. Peter looked at him in shock. "Where are you going?"

"First, I've got to check into my hotel. Then, I'm doing what anyone who people think is a god would do in this situation: I'm going to hunt a great big bloody monster and stick its head on a pike."

CHAPTER EIGHT: BUMP IN THE NIGHT

There was a hotel on O'Connell Street that didn't exist, unless you knew where to look for it. This confused a great many wizards on their first visit to Dublin, when they didn't know where to stay and had instead used modern systems of booking hotels. The Dagda Inn was a secret, dispensing so many distractions into the air that it put Kurt to shame, cloaked in every sort of protection spell and cloaking charm and warding device that ancient and modern wizardry could come up with.

It was part of a larger chain of hotels around the world, though they all went by different names to avoid confusion. They borrowed from local myths and stories, sometimes naming themselves after old gods, and other times naming themselves after modern legends. Detroit, for example, had named their branch The Franklin, after the soul singer, while London had named themselves The Pan, after Peter Pan.

There were rules to the hotels, which kept them safe and popular.

Anyone with an ounce of magical ability or affliction, whether they were a wizard or a werewolf or a wendigo, could book a room. There was always space at the hotels, though pre-booking was advised. The only exceptions were staff members of Damage Control; in an attempt to provide hospitality to those who might be somewhat undesirable in their nature, policing was forbidden. Trust in the fundamental safety of the hotel was vital.

Additionally, no one could bring about harm to anyone else in the hotel. This included the staff, the guests, or the spirits that lingered between the walls. Detection spells were in place for anyone who might accidentally overdo it when performing magic in their rooms, though the walls were properly warded just in case.

Demonic summonings were illegal, anyway, and by arrangement with Damage Control were banned from the hotels around the globe. The peace of mind provided by forbidding even minor summonings in the case of witchcraft and wizardry allowed everyone to sleep at night or day.

Everything else in the hotel fell under the same standards of modern hospitality. Stealing the towels was frowned upon. The minibar was too expensive. The restaurant was probably good enough that one needn't venture into the city. The staff would clean rooms in the morning, or at night if by request of certain nocturnal creatures of habit.

Kurt did not sleep in his room in the Dagda, no matter how much he wanted to. He had waited up for the sun to set and headed out, a vampire on his tail from the same floor that quickly headed in the direction of Temple Bar. Night in Dublin, in any other part of the city, was quiet. In London, people always filled the air with noise. There was always a party and always a tourist shouting blind drunk as they walked back to their hotel. There was always something to blame on a night without sleep.

It was more than just quietness. It was silence. Aside from traffic on the roads, and that mostly being buses, the city was silent.

Kurt walked slowly down Henry Street; by day it was loud and bustling, full of people, so many of them screaming, enough of them with special offers at random shopping carts that it was a headache waiting to happen. Every day, Kurt felt a little bit older his current incarnation.

There were still people on Henry Street that night. Aside from a couple of rough sleepers, the rest were huddled together groups of five or six people, looking over their shoulders and whimpering softly as they walked.

There was a perverse fear in Dublin. "They don't even know what's wrong," Kurt muttered to himself. He knelt beside a woman sleeping under the shelter of a pharmacy. She was still awake, eyes wide open. "Are you alright?" he asked her.

"Do I look alright?"

He guessed she was about his age, though she looked a few years older. The streets had worn her down. "I just mean that you a look a little on edge," Kurt replied. "Is there something on your mind? Something I can help you with?"

"Unless you can stop people disappearing, no," she snapped. He didn't move. "What?"

"It's why I'm here," he told her. "To figure out what's going on, and put an end to it. It's my job."

"You get paid to stop homeless people going missing?" He shook his head. "Then it's not a job. It's charity." She sat upright. "We don't have anywhere to go. People are too scared to leave the area. The charities can't do anythin' to help us out." She picked up a cup from behind her. "Damn it, cold."

Kurt reached out a hand. "May I?" He grabbed the cup and held on until steam began to pour from the top again. "Pretend you didn't see that," he told her with a wink.

She sipped her drink. "Better than a bleedin' microwave, anyway. Cheers." She drank while it was still hot, and so she could avoid talking. Finally, after a few minutes of him kneeling beside her in silence, she added, "People feel sorry for us, but they don't help us. That's what we have to deal with every day, and it's only gotten worse."

"I wish I could do more than heat up tea," he told her. "I'm trying."

"I believe yeh," she replied. "Look, they said Philly's mad. He says he saw a monster the other night. He was drunk, but…" She shook her head. "It's stupid, never mind."

"You believe him," Kurt said firmly. "Stay on this part of the street, that's all I'll say. The river isn't safe."

"Thanks, mister," she muttered. "Now, would you feck off so I'm not attracting attention?" She smiled when she said it. Her teeth were yellowing, but otherwise clean. Kurt wondered who let her brush them, who let her shower, and take care of herself. Who helped when no one would? He stood up with more difficulty than he ought to have had, his legs still recovering from the chase through London; he really had gone too far, then.

"Take care of yourself," he told her. He took out his wallet when he had his back to her, and most of the few notes he had disappeared before his eyes. She wouldn't notice them with her change until the next morning, he thought, but he doubted she would have taken the money from him directly. Besides, he thought, he couldn't afford to do it for everyone.

He visited a few others along the street, before turning to walk down the road where he'd been hit by a car. It looked different at night. There were fewer people. That didn't stop someone sitting outside a corner shop, of course, but rough sleepers would take what shelter they could get.

"How're you doing, sir?" the man said to Kurt.

"You stole my line," Kurt replied, and the man laughed. "What are you doing all the way over here?" he asked.

The man looked up defiantly. "It's my spot. It's always my spot if I can't get a hostel." Kurt could feel the age in his words. *Always* was a very long time to be sleeping on the streets. "Hostels were full tonight, everyone trying to get indoors. So I'm here."

"Are you going to be alright?" Kurt asked him.

"I've eaten," the man replied. "The place across the road gives me leftovers, sometimes. The shop will give me a cup of tea in the morning. I think it's one of the blokes who works there paying for it, but still. I'll be fine."

Kurt sighed. "You're not worried about what's been going on?"

The man stood up, leaning against the wall for balance. "If I worried every time something bad happened on the streets of Dublin, I'd never sleep. I'd be up every night. The only difference is, now people are paying attention, and everyone's sayin' the same thing: Philly was drunk, so don't believe him."

"And you don't believe him because of that?"

"He was drunk!" The man scooped up a bottle from the ground. It was impossible to tell whether it was water or vodka, without the smell. "You just don't know with people."

Kurt was about to argue, about to say something - anything - to get the man to move away from the spot, when they were interrupted. Rather, the man's screams cut Kurt off from speaking any more. A tentacle had the man by the ankle, and was pulling him through the air towards the river.

This was beyond the reach Kurt had anticipated for the monster. With heavy legs he ran after the man, a fireball burning in his right hand. He threw it just as the creature emerged over the edge of the wall by the river, twice the size as it had been before. The fireball collided with it, sizzling against its reptilian chest that was half scales and half water. It screamed in defiance, but it didn't deter. The man was still zooming towards it.

"All or nothing," Kurt said to himself, slapping his hands against the ground. A bolt of white light shot down the road, quicker than Kurt could have run. It exploded into a wall of solid light, visible for barely a second, severing the tentacle that was pulling the homeless man. The man's velocity hadn't decreased, and he was still zipping towards the water, still on the monster's menu for the night.

Kurt didn't have any other choice. He reached out with all of his will, catching the man with the magical equivalent of telekinesis, and swinging him back around in the other direction. He had to be quick and careful, trying to avoid tentacles along the way. The man came crashing down to the ground beside Kurt, a little bit sore, somewhat nauseated, and alive.

"What was that?"

"That's the monster trying to eat you," Kurt told him. "Now get out of here, and stay away." The man grabbed his belongings in a hurry, something Kurt almost begrudged him for, and ran stumbling away from the Liffey. "He better keep his mouth shut, or things are going to get worse around here," Kurt muttered to himself.

He moved closer to the monster. It was worse up close, flesh practically melting while it tried to figure out whether it was a solid creature or a construct of water. It screamed at Kurt, and he knew that this time he couldn't put out enough distractions into the air to stop people noticing. He needed to rely on the old trick of rational minds protecting people from unexplainable dangers.

"Just you and me, now," he scowled. "Come, show me what you've got."

He was met, immediately, with three tentacles swinging downwards like hammers. Without time to put up a magical shield, Kurt was forced to tear up the road in front of him as a defense. Stone and tarmac rose into a half dome over him, immediately cracked by the force of the monster's assault. Kurt swore to himself, diving out from under the shield as it was struck again. Rubble exploded, and the monster cried victory.

Kurt launched several fireballs in quick succession, but they were avoided with such ease that the Magic Man began to doubt his aim. He thought about the Mind's Eye, and whether it was disrupting him again.

"Not now, alright?" he hissed.

He was wrong, he soon discovered. It wasn't the Mind's Eye that was the problem. It was an eye made from light on the monster's forehead, glowing green. He hadn't noticed it before, and maybe, he thought, it was because the creature hadn't needed it until now, but he could feel the sort of magic needed for an eye like that. Reality was bending around it, space and time folding and unfolding unpredictably.

"Gods help me, that thing can see into the future." The tentacles moved quicker, now, more precise swings coming down on Kurt. There was only one defence against this sort of assault: a random barrage of spells, whenever he felt danger was imminent. He couldn't think. He couldn't do anything but push through the intention of stopping the tentacles, one way or another, from grabbing him.

On one side, the air froze, bringing an ice sculpture smashing to the ground. On the other, the road swallowed the tentacle, sharp teeth made from brick snapping shut around the creature. Light burned away three consecutive assaults, and a blade of air sliced through another. Still they kept coming, a seemingly unending number of weapons for the monster to use.

Finally, it connected, grabbing Kurt's leg and sweeping him backwards off his feet. The ground slammed up on either of the tentacle, stopping it in place, but more were on their way. Kurt had to be quick. He grabbed at the watery flesh, a vice-like grip squeezing his leg to the point that would have broken anyone else's bones already.

Direct contact with the monster was unpleasant. "You're trapped here," Kurt said to it. "Magic that controls time and space have made you a prisoner in the Liffey. Who would do this?" It screamed as it tried to break free from the grip the road had on it.

Time was running out. The monster, whatever it was, however it could see his movements, couldn't anticipate random actions. It was thrown off, for the time being. Kurt needed to act. His arms filled with a strength far greater than their size would ever allow, the same magic he'd used in the chase through London. He pulled at the tentacle, ripping it apart in one swift motion that left his arms tired.

He climbed to his feet quickly. "Can't do that again," he thought. He could barely raise his hands to throw out defensive spells as more tentacles lashed at him.

The whole fight was beginning to feel somewhat hopeless. He couldn't get close to the creature. He didn't know how to destroy it, never mind simply hitting it. Not without destroying half the city, at least.

He had one last trick up his sleeve, but he couldn't kill it this way. Still, he reasoned, better to live now and figure it out later. He clapped his hands together, pulling them apart slowly. Between them, a ring of light glowed, a magical looking glass the likes of which most wizards would baulk at for its unnecessary flare and showmanship. This was why most wizards, Kurt thought, weren't on international watchlists.

"Sometimes, you can't be afraid to show off," Kurt said with a grin, remembering the old words of a former teacher.

The looking glass separated him from the creature. Its attacks stopping immediately. Kurt knew he could only pull this off once. The monster wouldn't fall for it after tonight. But it was all he had. It was the only way he could survive the night.

Staring through the looking glass was to stare backwards through time itself. Retrocognitive magic had always been something of a speciality of Kurt's, something that he had taken to using more frequently in his detective work than he had ever anticipated. It was not a weapon, not in most cases, but here it was, the perfect defence.

While the monster was distracted, he ran. There was nothing else he could do. Without knowing its weakness, without getting close enough to hit the body more easily, he would remain on the defensive until his magic was all spent.

His head was pounding when he crashed through the entrance of The Dagda Inn. At least two more victims just in the time it took him to get back to O'Connell Street. He collapsed onto his bed, awake until the body count stopped rising, and until his guilt was overcome with exhaustion.

There were no dreams in Dublin, that night.

Paul Carroll

Chapter Nine: Déjà Dead

Sleep did not come easy, or stay for long. Though The Dagda Inn was a magical building, even it wasn't soundproofed against the armies of seagulls that flocked around Dublin. The birds stirred with the sunrise, creating a cacophony that could, in theory, actually wake the dead. It did little for Kurt's headache.

He tried to pretend he wasn't suffering, which sometimes worked, and showered. The hotel was much too nice for him, he thought. A normal wizard in his standing would have publicly derided himself for having such notions of grandeur and pomposity as to stay there, even if it was literally the only option in the country.

He struggled into a café for breakfast with Peter; he would have much rathered the hotel food, but he didn't fancy explaining who Peter was at eight in the morning.

The fortune teller looked tired. "I was up all night with the noise," Peter told him. "Do you know how many people..?"

Kurt shook his head. "I stopped counting. It was too much."

"So you didn't get it then. That's a fair summary." Kurt's hand slammed down on the table. "Sorry, I didn't mean it like that."

"I almost died last night, do you know that?" Peter shook his head. "Bloody psychics. You lot only ever look for what suits you." He wolfed down a piece of dry toast, chewing with more ferocity than was necessary. "The monster can see into the future. Maybe just a little. Maybe just enough to know how not to die and who to eat without being caught. I couldn't get close. I managed to save one man, but how many died after that?"

Peter pulled a newspaper from his bag. "Do you want the actual answer?" He spread the story out on the table. "Five more homeless men, four of them on the south side of the river. And three others, two women and a man out for a few drinks. There's no stopping some people, I guess."

Kurt wanted to say *Unless you're a giant lizard monster with a million tentacles*, but he restrained himself. "All confirmed missing?"

"All of them," Peter told him. "There was a ninth person who backed up the story from that bloke a few days ago."

"Philly," Kurt said. "A drunk, but not an idiot. Any mention of me in there?"

Peter scanned the paper. "I didn't see anything. I guess no one saw you."

"Someone saw me. The corroborator of Philly's story. He almost died. I saved him, and I saved myself, and that was all I managed. That thing is too quick, too unpredictable."

"One life saved is good, though, isn't it?"

Kurt frowned. "But how many others are going to get hurt now that someone else is saying there's a monster in the river? People believe that stuff, for better or for worse. There'll be a panic if anyone who doesn't sleep on the streets ever decides to back them up. Or," Kurt added with a grimace, "if it shows up where there are plenty of witnesses."

Peter tapped the newspaper on the table. "There's talk of a curfew, though. That might protect people."

"For a psychic, you're not very helpful," Kurt groaned. "Will it help or won't it? You have the power in you to know what will happen and when. You don't need to guess or posture. You won't change the future by telling me that a curfew won't save people. I'm already trying to finish this thing before that becomes necessary."

The Dubliner looked away bashfully. "You don't need to be a bully about it."

They ate in silence for a few minutes. Kurt supposed he ought to apologise, or feel guilty, but he couldn't think of any other way to clear the whole thing up with Peter.

"All I'm saying is, be mindful of choices already made," Kurt told him. "You can do great things if you understand where consequences come from and how the future gets shaped. Decisions change everything." He took the newspaper from Peter. "Like this stupid idea."

That caught Peter's attention again, and he looked back to Kurt. Anything but a conversation about the incorrect usage of his future vision was good enough for him. "What stupid idea?"

"Searching the river," Kurt muttered, reading through the story. "When are they planning this? It's not in the paper."

Peter blanched, but Kurt refused to break eye contact. With a sigh, he closed his eyes. "They don't know yet," he said. "Some people want to do it today, others want to be sure the missing people aren't just play acting." He stopped. "I guess they only mean the ones who weren't sleeping outside."

"And what happens if they start today or tomorrow?"

Peter shook his head. "Sorry, I can't look at that. Not again. Assume it'll be bad."

Bad wasn't the word for it. Kurt knew better than to underestimate the danger that they were all in. Even just sitting there for breakfast was going to be an issue in the long run, he thought. He needed to take action. *They* needed to take action, before even more people were killed.

"A search of the river will wake that thing up, I'm certain of it," Kurt said, before downing his tea. "It'll have a buffet prodding it, goading it, and it won't waste any time attacking. It can reach a long way with those tentacles, and there doesn't seem to be any end to them."

"Can't you just, I don't know, trap it in a magical bubble or something? Or freeze the water?"

Kurt missed the days of simple solutions. "I don't know what would happen if I froze the river, but I do know that it wouldn't last very long. And as for bubbling it up? I don't even know how big it is. At my peak, maybe I could manage it, but only if I can be sure it's not about to whack me aside. Or worse, eat me." He stared at the empty plate of his disappointing breakfast. "I can't use my most effective spells in this fight, Peter. They'll destroy half the city."

"You're exaggerating, right? Half the city?"

"You've never witnessed a man with my sort of arsenal letting loose," Kurt insisted. "Anyway, I don't think I'm quite *there* yet. There's a lot of energy involved, and a lot of emotion. It's going to take you to stop this."

"Me?" The fortune teller almost fell off his chair. "Why me? I'm useless in a fight. Someone once tried to beat me up for my lunch money in school and I gave him my homework journal as well. The one time I tried to stand up for myself, I accidentally punched a teacher in the face, and then a brick wall. I'm not a fighter."

Kurt raised his hands defensively. "I'm not looking for a fighter. I'm looking to nullify its foresight."

There was a story, once, of a war between wizarding families. It lasted for five generations, delayed at every stage by the complete inactivity of either side.

Both families had what they called in those days a Prophet, who were born in the third generations. They saw the future in different ways, and looked for different things, but the families could never act. Every time they moved to enter combat, one Prophet or the other would warn them away; their plan was, as a result of being foretold by the other Prophet, null and void.

Only when the fourth and fifth generations were marrying each other, and the fighting had been stopped for decades as a result of inactivity, did anyone realise that the war was over. By this point, the Prophets were old, and withered, and worn out from minding their grandchildren. The first died, and the second wept, but she never looked to the future again.

Kurt told Peter the tale, and the fortune teller rolled his eyes.

"Is that the sort of bedtime story you were reared on?"

"It's not a bedtime story, it's history," Kurt insisted. "And that's not the point. The point is, if you're telling me how and when the monster will attack one or both of us, I can stop it. I've already fought it using instinct alone. It'll stop trying to predict everything when it realises it's always going to be thwarted."

Peter took a deep breath, and asked, "And what if you're wrong?" He didn't wait for a response. "What if it kills me when it realises what I'm doing? Or just stops me talking?"

"I'll figure it out," Kurt snapped. "You'll be safe, I promise. I won't let it hurt you."

"I need to think about it," Peter responded. "It's a big ask, going out there. I'm not like you."

"You're not like anyone," Kurt quipped. "Give it a few hours. But be warned, Peter: if you're worried about using your newfound power for this, you might want to consider the idea that killing the monster will put an end to your precognitive days. Time magic is spilling out from that thing. I've got to believe there's a reason you can see the things you can, all of a sudden."

He stood up to leave, Peter fretting at the table at the dilemma. "Wait," he said quietly. "Take the newspaper with you. I have this feeling you're going to need it at some point."

"Is this a psychic thing?"

"Isn't it always?" he responded sheepishly.

The Liffey looked different during the day. There was an unsettling calm about it, like the water wasn't aware that there was a giant monster lurking beneath its surface. Kurt imagined he could see it, but he knew he was kidding himself. The monster in the Liffey was practically made from the water itself.

He could feel it, though. The magic that bound it together, the time magic that spilled from it, it gave off a distinct aura. Once he'd become familiar with it, there was no mistaking it. It was there, as close to asleep as it could get, and it was going to wake up again sooner than later to eat. Kurt knew, from the body count and from observations about it, that it would be bigger, and more dangerous.

He didn't know how to defeat it.

"Okay, let's look at this properly," he said to himself, and the Mind's Eye opened.

The magic was disconcerting to say the least. It covered the whole basin of the river, a mess of tentacles hiding the rest of the beast. Kurt's head swam with dizziness just from looking at it, and he almost wished he could look away.

There was always something else, though, something more, if a detective knew to keep looking. Along the bank of the river, where tentacles reached in case anyone dared enter the water, were symbols just like those he'd seen in the Thames.

"Two rivers, two cities, one giant monster, and one vanishing man," he summarised. "That makes for one unfinished case that I won't be paid for." He wondered, briefly, how Damage Control had dealt with Edward's body, but shook the thought from his head. Gary would have gotten someone specific on the case, someone who knew to deal with things properly and with respect. Edward may have hired Kurt, but before that he had known nothing about the magical world. He'd been blind to his impending death.

Kurt took the long way around the river, avoiding the three bridges that were now the property of the beast. There were no symbols in the water beyond the external bridges. Whatever the spells were for, they were limited to one small strip of water.

He called the hotel on a number with too few digits. The receptionist, an orc male, who'd considered Kurt some suspicion that morning, answered, asking him all sorts of questions about his identity and his room number and the sort of business he had in the city, until he was satisfied he could help.

"I need whatever old books on magical symbology you have in stock delivered to my room. I understand the hotel still runs a library service out of the Alexandria?"

The Hotel Alexandria was part of the hotel chain, located in Egypt. It was founded and named following the burning of the original library, and used as a *de facto* replacement for the magical community. Utilising new printing techniques and advanced teleportation spells, the library at the Hotel Alexandria was capable of loaning out copies of books that would have otherwise vanished, though they restricted the service to hotel clients. The books couldn't be removed, both by policy and by the combustion spells on every page, securing the Hotel Alexandria's reputation as world leader in both occult publishing and library management.

The orc knew all of this, but still groaned down the phone. "It'll just be a copy, you understand that right?"

"Yes yes, and completely unremovable. I wouldn't even attempt it. I have too much respect for the hotel to even consider it."

"So long as we're on the same page," the orc said with a gruff voice, and immediately started to laugh at his own joke. "We have a few titles that cover the greatest scope of symbols."

"Thank you, Mister…"

"O'Neill," the orc told him. "We're still in Ireland, we'll stick to our names." He hung up, and it took Kurt a few moments to process the call and figure out at what point he'd insulted the orc.

With a sigh, he left the Liffey and headed towards Peter's stall just off Moore Street. He'd been given vague directions, and always thought he was good at finding his way around, but it still took him twice as long as he expected to navigate the old city. Roads were thrown together roughly, as if the buildings were put in place first and someone only then remembered that they needed to be able to steer horses and carts around.

Moore Street was alive with activity, people shouting out special offers in cigarettes and bananas, while cars on one end of the street did their best to run over as few people as possible. Kurt found Peter's stall open.

The fortune teller was standing over his table, a letter in his hand. Kurt recognised the envelope, the same sort he'd found in Edward's apartment, and dragged Peter away. Peter dropped the letter from his hand just as the ink began to glow.

He fell on top of Kurt as the stall exploded.

It was no ordinary flame. Kurt could feel the darkness burning in it as it consumed Peter's livelihood, roaring like a demon soaked in holy water.

"Jesus Christ, what was that?" Peter screamed.

Kurt pushes him off and stood, watching the small stall burn away to nothing. "Hellfire," he responded. "You should be able to smell the sulphur in the air."

"Okay, but what *was* it?"

Where did he start? He didn't think Peter would fair too well at the mention of demons. He didn't think Peter needed an explanation about the source of Hellfire. "You want the truth? That was an assassination attempt, Peter. Someone wants you dead."

He rummaged around in his bag while Peter fanned himself. The stall was gone. No one seemed to have noticed. "I don't understand," Peter whimpered.

Kurt produced the page that he'd found in Edward's apartment. "Is this the symbol that you saw?" Peter nodded. "I was afraid of that. The same people who sent this sent one to my client in London. He died on the morning I came here. Burned to a crisp, and I couldn't smell the difference…"

"I don't know what you're talking about. Why would someone want me dead? I didn't do anything."

"I have a theory," Kurt told him. "I need more information, but I think the problems I had in London are connected to what's going on here." He looked around nervously. "It won't take long for them to realise that you're not dead. Come on, you're staying at my hotel room."

"I can't sleep at a time like this," Peter cried.

Kurt kept his mouth shut. There had almost been the possibility that Peter would never sleep again. Something connected Edward and Peter, something had made both of them call him. Kurt just needed to join the right dots.

Paul Carroll

CHAPTER TEN: MISSED CONNECTIONS

For his safety and to give him a chance to let the shock wear off, Peter slept on Kurt's bed at the Dagda Inn. He snored, which forced Kurt to throw a silencing spell around him, and he sprawled out so that Kurt couldn't even sit on the bed. He was in an armchair, instead, looking out over O'Connell Street any time his attention slipped from his work. He had the newspaper on his lap, scorched at the edges by Hellfire.

One page stuck out at an awkward angle, the whole thing falling apart after losing a staple. Kurt tore it out and discarded the rest of the mess. "*Missed Connections?* I didn't think they did these things anymore," he said to himself. He skimmed through the letters, most of them for someone on the bus, or the bloke on the Luas with the gym bag and the accent, or the woman in the coffee place with the big boots. Kurt wasn't sure if it was a typo. His attention was drawn, instead to The London Boy in Town.

He wasn't going to immediately kid himself into thinking that it was meant for him, but he couldn't think of another reason why Peter would have given him the paper.

To the London Boy in Town; you really gave them Hell yesterday at the barbeque place, but you left something behind. Not to be too Forward, but it's vital you get your hands on it. I'll be keeping an Eye on the Time until we meet again. Kisses, Mad to Miss You.

"She wouldn't." He read it over and over again. "She really wouldn't. Not her." He looked into the mirror hanging on the wall, and the Mind's Eye flared. "Kisses? Really?"

The Eye burned, and Kurt wanted to close it. It stayed open just long enough for an envelope to fall out of thin air, dropping onto his lap, and the pain left. He felt something like the idea of laughter at the back of his mind.

It was a little-known secret that Madame Madness enjoyed toying with people. Kurt knew it. He had always known it. He had never known her to think it wise to toy with him, once he'd come into his power. She was smart enough not to. He glared at the mirror. She must have known, he thought, that he would leave something behind at Edward's apartment.

He sighed, and picked up the envelope. It was addressed to him, in the hotel room, in messy handwriting. He knew without having anything to compare to that it had come from Edward Armstrong, and he guessed that it had been written before he died. "He knew all along," Kurt muttered. He opened the envelope gently. Whatever anxiety Edward had been suffering from must have abated for long enough that he could gather his thoughts.

Dear Mister Crane,

I have spent the last three years of my life thinking about death. Anxiety induced suicidal ideation, my doctor said. Until recently, I didn't really believe any of the images in my head would become a reality. I'm less certain now. While waiting for you to return, everything began to make sense again. I only hope I can be standing in front of you while you read this, so we can figure out the next step together.

This feels strange to write, but I think I had time backwards in my head. I blame the anxiety. When I hired you to figure out who was following me, for what felt like days, it was just my brain putting everything in the wrong order. YOU were the person who was following me before I hired you. You just hadn't done it yet.

I have spent the last few hours wondering if hiring you invited some sort of danger upon myself, or if you're the only one who could hope to make sense of all of this. I have a feeling that other people are better suited for stopping what's wrong with me, and others are better at fighting off rogue wizards and explaining the magical community and beating back monsters in the dead of night, but none of those people can put all the pieces together.

I hired my own stalker, but I hired the best man for the job. No matter what happens, I wanted to make sure you got paid.

Something bad is coming, Mister Crane, and I don't think I'm going to survive this. I think, for once, the image in my head is the real and certain future, and I don't think I'll remember when the time comes what to do to protect myself.

Please don't blame yourself. Just do the job you were meant to do. Save the world, Mister Crane, and save the next guy. If I'm right, and I probably am, two out of three people in this case will be dead before you read this letter. Someone started all of this. Find them. Stop them.

And if you ever find the person responsible for doing this to me, try not to blow up half a city.

Your would-be friend, Edward.

Kurt folded it up again, quietly. He was not used to reading people's last words. He was not used to being around after people had just died. He grieved in dreams and nightmares, years later, after he'd died.

He was always the sacrifice. He was always the last victim. He couldn't deal with there being someone to mourn, especially not someone he barely knew. But maybe, he thought, maybe there was some truth to Edward's sign off. Maybe, in the infinite possibilities presented by the unfolding of space-time in every decision, maybe he was friends with Edward somewhere. Maybe Edward hadn't died.

He looked into the mirror again. He thought about what he would say to Madame Madness, if she were still listening.

He thought about how he would criticise her Missed Connections letter, or how he would thank her for delivering the letter, even if she hated to see him.

"Maybe we can get along after all," he said to her.

No response came. He hadn't expected one, either, but it would have been nice. He hid the letter in his bag, lest Peter read it.

"Two dead already," he muttered. "Two out of three. Edward, Peter, and... someone else." He racked his brain. He didn't know the third person. He hadn't met them yet, and he never would. Peter wasn't dead. Peter was the last one to protect. He looked to his sleeping charge, and tried not to worry. If Peter didn't want to help, he would have to figure out another way to blind the beast from his attacks. He would have to figure out how to battle it alone.

The whole world was at stake, and Dubliners were still too busy complaining about an abundance of Italian language students to notice. If push came to shove, there could be no sugar-coating reality for the fair city.

There was a monster in the river, and no one could hide from it anymore.

Creating one-use spells out of a few basic raw materials was a long and exhausting process. The long term benefit was that the spells wouldn't require much more than a spark of intent to get them going again, which was much easier than, for instance, creating a freezing spell to cover half the width of the Liffey. Kurt was under no false impression that it would contain the monster, but at the very least it might slow it down.

He was halfway through crafting a binding spell when there was a knock on his door.

"Alexandria Books," a voice called from the other side. "Half a dozen titles under order from the Magic Man." Kurt grimaced at the moniker, but the hotel refused to relay a request using his real name.

He opened the door to a pixie. She was slight and short and twinkling where she floated, and there was no reasonable way she could have made as much noise as she had. With the blink of an eye, she resembled an ordinary human girl, dressed in the hotel's uniform. Kurt tried his best to conceal a frown.

"Everything alright, sir?" she asked him.

"Yes, sorry. Didn't mean to stare. You can just call me Kurt."

She shook her head. "I don't think so, no. I just need you to sign for the books so I can leave." A scroll appeared in the air beside her. Signing books out from Alexandria meant placing a magical seal on the parchment with one's thumb. The paper did all the work. It was a way to ensure no one could truly lie about their identity. The Library always knew the truth.

Kurt obliged, and the scroll vanished. The pixie turned to depart. "Wait," he said to her. "Did I offend you?"

"Well, the staring wasn't very pleasant, but no. The truth is, sir, anyone who's heard of you, which is just about everyone, knows to avoid you. Now, please just let me do my job." He nodded, and with a click of her fingers, she was gone.

The books sat on his dressing table. He sat down in front of them, nursing a headache. The Mind's Eye was beginning to cause trouble again, he realised.

"Who was the girl?" Peter asked. He rolled upright, groggy from his sleep.

"Book delivery," Kurt muttered.

"She didn't look very interested in talking to you." Kurt shot him a glare. "Just an observation. It's weird, of course. You're a good-looking guy. There's no reason she shouldn't have been even a little bit interested."

"It's complicated, Peter. Sometimes reputation comes before looks."

Peter laughed, as if forgetting his near death experience. "Oh, a heartbreaker. Known for getting around, then?"

"What? No. Gods, people these days. You're worse than when there was nothing to do *but* shag. I've a habit of getting people killed. She didn't want anything to do with that." Peter looked back at him with wide eyes. "For a psychic, you really get surprised a lot, Peter."

The fortune teller stood up, arms crossed, in a huff. "I'll have you know that I prefer to live in the now. Future vision is great, but what's the point in doing anything if you already know what's going to happen? Life is all about surprises. Like this." He stood at the window, staring out onto Dublin. "There's no hotel here."

"Not one you can see," Kurt corrected him. "Enjoy the view. I've got work to do." He began flicking through the books, looking for anything that might resemble the symbols in the water. He had a rough sketch beside him to judge by. He had always enjoyed drawing. It was a human sort of magic, to take an image from one place and put it on paper with nothing more than a pencil or some ink.

Peter tried to talk to him several times, after which Kurt threatened to feed him to the monster in the Liffey.

The problem with old books, even new copies of them, was that they were never in the first language people knew.

One tome, which detailed European symbology and its practical uses, had been written in Latin. The book, *Magna Typicus*, was the cornerstone of modern magic, and had led to the rise of magical powers around the world. Anyone who knew anything about magical history and the academic study of magic knew something about the book, though the level of detail contained within its pages was usually too much for any wizard to learn in a single lifetime.

Another book, describing the use of demonic symbols in magic, was in Sanskrit; its cover contained a skull, but no title. It was read according to reputation. The book inspired the rise of necromancy, provided instructions on summoning and defending against demons, and warned against certain Greater Demons. Kurt had read it several times over already, so he needed only to flick through for illustrations that might provide some insight into the river spells. He didn't fancy revision on demonology at the time.

A third book was in ancient Greek, with notes in Spanish - known on the continent as *Padre del Paraíso* - describing symbols relating to godhood and the creation and disassembly of Pantheons. Kurt had never looked at it before, but he knew about it. The author had lived for two hundred years, exploring new lands before the official discovery of the New World. He had collected every single facet of information about gods around the world. He had been an expert. And, Kurt thought with a frown, he was anonymous. No one ever remembered the men and women who did some of the most important work.

The fourth text – *Middengeard Bealucræft* - was written in old English, describing attempts at incorporating symbols and magic from foreign lands with those from the Royal library. The author was long suspected to have been a vampire, too stubborn to change how he wrote during the evolution of the English language over the centuries. That, or he had been trying to toy with people. The book was, Kurt thought, the most entitled piece of magical literature in existence, bred from a desire to control the known world. It covered everything from hoodoo and shamanism to witch doctors and ancient medicine, all the time focusing on the rise of the British Empire. It was one of the more recent books on symbology that carried any sort of academic importance, if one could overlook its politics. Kurt felt distinctly un-British reading it.

The fifth book dealt with Enochian symbology, written in ink that changed language every few seconds. It would change from Hebrew to Cantonese to French and even to English, swapping between half a dozen dead languages every minute. Only a handful of people had ever read it cover to cover. No one knew the author, though Kurt could have taken a guess. He once declared that it had come from Metatron himself, the Scribe of God, and had been hushed for daring to suggest that.

The sixth and final book, dating from the earliest point in human magic, described the use of symbols around the world and their relationship with the fundamental forces that governed the universe. The four basic elements from which all life sprang - fire, earth, water, and air - were alongside symbolic understandings of time, space, gravity, magnetism, radiation and energy. However anyone understood the world, it had been recorded.

Kurt always had the impression that the first wizards were learned men, gifted with a new way of looking at the world before they could cast a simple spell. There was no way, he reasoned, that men who were otherwise primitive people could have known so much.

He also, sometimes, assumed it was all a lie.

"You look miserable reading those," Peter observed. Kurt tried to ignore him. "I bet you anything that you won't know what you're looking for until you stop looking so hard."

"Is this a psychic thing again?"

"This is an Irish thing," Peter said. "The psychic part of me says that you should just flick open a few of the books onto a random page because you're annoyed at me for opening my gob again."

Kurt wanted to slam his head against the table. Instead, he threw the books open. "There, happy?"

"You tell me."

Kurt looked down at the books. "Water magic, combining spells from different regions…" He quickly began copying down images from the books onto blank sheets of paper, folding them over and trying his best to join the lines together. "Peter, we have a problem."

The psychic raised his hands defensively. "I didn't do anything."

"Not you. Not yet. It's the rivers. The symbols in the rivers are like… I don't know, joined, two halves of the same spell. It's teleportation magic, on a big scale. The sort that can send something big, if it has enough power."

"So what are you thinking?"

"The monster in the Liffey, it's both the battery and the object to be sent. It's feeding so much for a reason." He closed the books. He already had his answers. "This sort of magic hasn't been done before on this scale. This could tear up the universe as we know it."

Peter half laughed. "Don't you think you're being a little bit dramatic?"

Looking him right in the eye with a deadpan expression, Kurt said, "Prove me wrong." He was not fond of putting pressure on people, but Peter made it difficult to avoid. They needed to know what the stakes were. It came down to figuring out if energy would best the spent dismantling the spell in the Liffey or fighting the beast that would supercharge it. The only person with any direct connection to any of it, as far as Kurt could tell, was the man standing before him. Only Peter, at this point in time and in this city, could tell Kurt whether they were all doomed, or whether the monster would simply wreak havoc.

The problem was that Peter couldn't stand the sight of death. His first couple of involuntary experiences since gaining his foresight had been more than enough. He sat down on the bed. "I don't want to. I don't want to see what that thing will do. I don't want to stop seeing the future. I don't want any of this. I just want to run my little stall, help a few people, rig the lottery every now and then so I can move out of my council house, and maybe find a nice guy to date. It's not fair."

It wasn't. Kurt could agree with him there. And he knew there wasn't anything he could say to convince Peter otherwise.

After a few minutes of silence, Peter asked, "What exactly do you want me to check? Tell me now before I change my mind."

There was one vital thing he needed to know. "What will happen if the spell activates before we can stop that thing in the river?"

Peter closed his eyes. He hoped, for a moment, that he wouldn't always need to whenever he looked into the future. Then, he looked.

"Dublin is dead," he said. "The city is empty, its buildings in ruin, its people devoured or gone." Kurt wanted to ask questions, but it seemed to him that Peter was in a trance. He began transcribing. "The beast consumed hundreds before it disappeared, a flash of light and an explosion so terrible that no one could stop it."

He whispered under his breath, "I don't want to do this, Kurt."

He was pulled back in before Kurt could say anything. "When it arrived in London, it began to feed more quickly. It changed. It mutated. It multiplied. Parts of it took to the land, great beasts with an impossible hunger. They hunted. They killed. They could not be stopped. Help came, soldiers with guns and soldiers with magic, and all fell. The Reapers were powerless to stop it. One by one they fell. There was only one option. One last resort."

Kurt knew the name he was about to speak. "Kerubiel." The leader of the Cherubim. The last resort in every world-ending event was an angel smiting, right from the source.

"London is no more."

Peter collapsed onto the bed. Kurt rushed to his side to see if he was okay. "A little dizzy," Peter said to him. "How was that?"

"You did great. But the outlook isn't too good." He poured Peter a glass of water, and sat by the window. Dublin looked so peaceful. "No one will help here. It's just us. Damage Control aren't monitoring the city. The Reapers aren't aware of this. Or if they are, they aren't acting on it."

"So, what's going to happen?"

Kurt emptied his bag of the protection charms he'd bought to save Edward. "I get to work, and then we stop this thing turning Dublin into a feeding ground."

Paul Carroll

Chapter Eleven: The Once and Future Beast

Nightfall brought with it a tension that couldn't be contained. Even in the relative safety of The Dagda Inn, the patrons were struggling to deal with the atmosphere that had fallen over the city. There was no talk of a monster without a name, or the disappearances in Dublin that had all but taken over the media. There was no mention at all of how the Magic Man and his new friend left the hotel against the best advice of the orc at the front desk.

The duo left just as the sun set, and not a moment too soon. Peter had been reluctant to check when the waters would be disturbed, not that it mattered. The city was empty.

"I thought the curfew hadn't come into effect yet," Kurt said as they walked down an abandoned Henry Street. None of the rough sleepers from before were present, which felt like something of a relief. "Where is everyone?"

"I can see the future, Kurt, I'm not omniscient." He stopped walking. "But I think people just opened their doors to them. This is Dublin. People look after each other. They'll throw them out first thing in the morning, but at least they'll be able to stay safe."

Kurt almost choked on a single laugh that escaped from his mouth. "Is anywhere safe?" Peter still hadn't moved. "It was a rhetorical question, Peter. I know the dangers we're facing. I know just how far it extends. In theory."

Without people in the way or people to talk to, it didn't take more than a couple of minutes to walk the length of

Henry Street until the reached the Jervis Shopping Centre. Places like that, Kurt thought, they were the safety bunkers. Not the hotel, with its barriers to prevent detection, but the shopping centres with food and multiple exists and the capacity to hold hundreds of people. The familiarity people had with the building could be used to craft protective barriers around the perimeter. Its height allowed for the weak or elderly to stay out of range of the beast's attacks if it ever breached one of the entrances.

Maybe, if it all came down to it, it could be a refuge. For now, it was where they needed to turn. Heading towards the river made Peter so nervous he almost threw up. He reminded himself of his Finglas roots, his Dublin sensibilities, and his Irish capacity to hold back vomit unless absolutely necessary.

Still walking, he said to Kurt, "It can reach across the Luas tracks now." That didn't give them a lot of time, and it put a huge distance between Kurt's attacks the beast's body. "I won't be able to keep up with you if you go charging in, remember that."

"I know, I know. Just stay verbal. Every command has to be clear and concise." He flexed his hands, charging them with magical energy to have at the ready. "Predict enough that it gives up trying to figure out my next move with its own precognition. I can handle the rest, I think."

He knew he wasn't being especially reassuring, but that wasn't his job right now. He was an artillery weapon, and Peter had to order it which way to shoot. It couldn't become more complicated than that, or they would fail.

They arrived at the Luas tracks. "Here goes nothing," Kurt said, and stepped slowly and purposefully across the road. He could feel the beast rising from the river even from that distance. "Peter, whenever you're ready."

Three tentacles rose into the air, each one splitting at along the top into three or four other tentacles. Peter hadn't told him it would happen. Kurt could only hope that this was part of the plan.

Three deadly whips were swinging down at Kurt, each one wider than his arm. He held his breath, waiting for impact or for Peter to finally give him some indication about what to do.

"Any time now."

"The right is coming for me. The other two are going to try stop you from protecting me." He stopped walking. "Jesus, Kurt I can't do this."

"No quitting on me now, Peter," Kurt responded. He had to clear his mind. He knew his targets, but the monster didn't know what he might do to hit them.

Impact was imminent.

"Peter, duck," Kurt yelled. The tentacles came thrashing down together, just as chains exploded out of the ground, a dozen or more of them stabbing through the tentacles with pointed blades at their tips. The chains spouted from small glowing portals, burning with yellowish fire. It was a spell that Kurt hadn't used in the longest time, a practice that had been instrumental in his studies of magic. The Chained Mage had shown him the physical links as a means to understanding the metaphorical ones.

Neither Peter nor the river beast had seen them coming. The tentacles writhed against the metal, stuck in place and burning.

"What the heck was that?" Peter screamed. "You almost hit me with one of those."

"Next attack Peter. We'll talk about the meaning of the word 'duck' later, when we're not dead."

The fortune teller sighed, but he could at least move again. Adrenaline was finally doing its job. "You've caught it off guard. It's going to try attack along the other side of the street, this time."

"And if I block that one as well?"

"It'll sever its own arm," Peter told him, with a grimace upon his face. "It's a thing octopuses do when they're trapped."

The second tentacle came down upon them quickly, four tips shooting downwards from the sky.

"All on you, and then the third arm will hit the buildings," Peter called.

"Clever girl," Kurt muttered. He raised his arms defensively, and pieces of the road burst upwards, stone jaws biting at the tentacles. At the last second, they exploded, ripping the arm to pieces.

There was no time for celebration. He dove against the nearby wall, clapping his hands against the stone. Light shot up the full height of the building. The third main tentacle collided with the light; it was like a firework going off overhead, filling the street and the Liffey with dazzling light.

Peter caught up with him as they reached the shop where Kurt had intercepted the previous night's first attack. The tentacle stretching the length of the road on the other side fell limp, and crashed to the ground. It burned with a green light, sizzling away in a cloud of steam.

"Are you safe right beside me?"

"As safe as I can be," Peter said weakly. "Give me one of the premade spells in your bag. Any of them. Don't make a choice."

Kurt grinned. "Now you're getting it." He dug into his bag. He knew that it wouldn't be enough, but it could possibly save Peter's life. He imagined the psychic could see something, some vague possibility in an undecided future, and would rather the safety of a limited arsenal than to be caught unprotected.

"Jesus that thing is huge," Peter whispered, and Kurt's attention returned to the river. The lizard half of the monster was more than twice its previous size. Big enough to swallow a man whole, Kurt thought.

It roared at them, and Kurt began to worry. "We're going to draw too much attention if we don't finish this soon," he said. "What do we do?"

"We get closer," Peter told him. "And we pray that I can keep up with its future vision."

They were allowed to get closer, which did little to calm Kurt's nerves. The monster wanted this, he thought, or it couldn't tell what they were planning anymore. He hoped he was right, or they were in for a shock that even Peter couldn't predict if he wasn't paying enough attention.

Up close, and they were truly close to the beast now, the beast was a nightmare made flesh. It's lizard top-half was glistening as it shifted from a watery state to scales and back again, constantly in flux. Its underbelly looked like a weak spot, if it had any. Kurt couldn't imagine how a heart would work in something like this.

At the waist, from what Kurt could see of the waist as the creature loomed over them, it was like the tentacled-half was stitched on, and poorly at that. It had something resembling hips, before the tentacles seemed to take over. They were mostly water at this end of the body, as if the river itself were pushing the creature up enough for it to threaten the magician and his precognitive apprentice.

Peter gasped, stuck for words, struggling to vocalise a warning in time. Kurt let instinct take over. Fire poured from one hand, roaring as it scorched an incoming tentacle, while a blast of black light, an absence made from magic, shot from the other.

The second tentacle, subjected to dark magic, became like an infection. Kurt and Peter watched as it spread down one side of the monster. Kurt didn't need magic or the Mind's Eye to understand that he had caused it pain.

"What was that?" Peter asked.

"Something evil," Kurt muttered. "Dark magic. I didn't mean to. I really shouldn't have done that."

"But it worked!" The fortune teller seemed ecstatic, and distracted.

"Peter, look out," Kurt shouted, as an infected tentacle whistled towards him, poked with holes from Kurt's spell.

As he dived for cover, Peter threw the charm he'd taken from Kurt. A small vortex opened overhead, sucking in the corrupted elements of the monster.

"Now Peter, how do I stop it?"

The fortune teller kept his head buried in his arms. "I can't. I'm sorry Kurt. I need this."

"Damn it, we don't have time. It's hurt. It's distracted. It has to be now."

The creature had other ideas. It screamed one last time before sinking into the water again. Kurt didn't know for sure, but he guessed that it was still alive, and it would be back.

"Did you see that?" Kurt heard a woman say.

People were approaching, now, from every side and every street. The noise of the battle, the light show that Kurt had put on, the screaming, it had drawn a crowd.

The magician ran to Peter's side. There was no time for distractions. They were already seen. Instead, he placed a blur over their faces, the way he'd seen television shows do it for years. People looked at them curiously, but Kurt wasn't going to allow them to become trapped.

"This will hurt," Kurt whispered. His strengthening spells flooded his body, and he was suddenly unsure who was going to suffer more from this, him or Peter. He lifted the other man up into his arms and leapt over the crowd. He ran until they were out of sight around the corner and dropped to the ground, landing on top of Peter. Distractions poured out around them, to conceal them from further attention.

The effort, especially following a fight, caused Kurt to empty the contents of his stomach.

"You want to explain what just happened there?" he asked Peter.

"I'm sorry. I said I was sorry. I don't know what I'd do without this ability. I've never felt more like myself, except for when I came out to my mam. You don't know what it's like, to suddenly be so sure of everything."

Kurt growled, his stomach twisting. "The way things went tonight is not okay, Peter." He sat back against the wall. "I used spells that are almost as dangerous to me as they were to that *thing*, and you can't tell me how to stop it because you're afraid to lose something you just got?"

"I said-"

"That you're sorry. And I accept that. But if you care so much about your new ability, why didn't you use it to tell me that people were coming?" Peter looked up at him, finally. The colour had drained from Kurt's face. "Do you know how hard I work to stop people finding out about me? About the magical community? Damage Control may hate me, but at least I *try* to stick to that rule."

The world was spinning, a sensation not helped by the presence of the Mind's Eye trying to force itself open. The last thing he needed, he thought.

"You owe me breakfast, since I just lost the excuse for a dinner I had earlier." He tried massaging his temples to nurse a rising headache. "Before you ask me if anywhere is open, I want you to remember two things: I'm not from here, and I'm not the psychic. Just find somewhere close."

Close was a ten minute walk back to the hotel when neither Peter's psychic powers or ability to search for anything online turned up any results. Under threat of Kurt passing out on the floor, the hotel provided them with a private space in the dining area.

"We're only really serving dinner," the woman who served them said. "The nocturnal guests aren't fond of grease or grain."

Peter looked nervously at Kurt. "Two steaks, then? And some water."

"A good call. I'll have the same. Medium well, please," Kurt added. The woman left, confused and uncertain. "This is a mess, Peter. People could die because you wouldn't act. *I* could have died. And then you. Horribly. Painfully."

"Are you trying to scare me?"

Kurt glared at Peter. "If I was trying to scare you, you'd be scared." He tried to relax himself, his features calming. "I'm trying to keep you and as many other people as possible alive."

The server left them with their food. Peter's stomach turned. Kurt ate quickly; there was nothing but meat on the plates. The nocturnal guests, Kurt assumed, were trying *not* to eat the city. He cleared his own plate in silence, before Peter passed over a third steak. Halfway through, the water emptied, Kurt stopped.

"Much better," he sighed. He looked at the fortune teller with sympathy. "It's time you heard a story about a slightly younger man in a slightly older body, and the woman he lost." Peter nodded, seeming to understand. "It was the 1980s. I guess you were just a kid. I was, I think, about this age when I decided I wanted to marry her. I was working, she was visiting from America again, and we were in love."

"What happened? Did she…"

Kurt shook his head. "I did. Nasty fight. Lots of blood. She got away, thankfully, but that's hardly enough. Not when I came back as a baby the next day, not when I had to grow up all over again with this perfect image of her in my head."

He fell silent. He hadn't thought about telling anyone about this who didn't already know.

"Something happened to her, and we can't get close. And I was still a teenager for a long time. I looked so much younger than her the last time I saw her. I couldn't do that to her. She knew that. But we still loved each other. She knew everything about me, even - no, especially - the things I was ashamed of. She was everything to me."

"The point, Peter, is that sometimes you have to let go of the thing you love. Sometimes it can cause you more pain and sorrow than you know how to process."

"You want me to let go?"

"Read the future and see what I want," Kurt told him dryly.

There was only one way to beat the beast. There was only one future in which they succeeded without the assistance of an angel. There was only one way to stop the world as they knew it from ending.

Paul Carroll

Chapter Twelve: The Rueful Stream

The world shook at noon; this was not a metaphor. Kurt, resting in the armchair in the hotel room, fell to the floor with something that could roughly be called a thump and could in no way be described as graceful. Peter, meanwhile, was thrown so forcefully from the bed that he felt like he might have broken something.

Kurt swore, which had the effect of setting the carpet alight. "Peter, get up and stop whining," he shouted. "Something's gone wrong."

"You don't bleedin' say."

Kurt grabbed his bag and threw Peter's jacket at him. "Don't you feel that in the air? Can't you see what's going on?" Peter gaped at him. "For gods' sake, Peter, look into the future."

The fortune teller obliged, and immediately let out a gasp. "The Liffey. Someone's car is about to get eaten."

"No time, then. Get up. Let's go. Emergency exit." He wrapped his arm under a complaining Peter's armpits and hefted him as he jumped through the window. The glass didn't so much as smash as move out of the way. The Dagda Inn was not especially fond of people abusing their charms in this fashion, but they were more realistic about their incapacity to replace windows without being seen. They floated the three storeys to the ground, and Kurt let Peter down.

"Never, ever throw me out a window again," Peter warned.

Kurt ignored him, taking off on a slow jog as people noticed their sudden materialisation on O'Connell Street. Peter followed him as quickly as he could. People moved out their way, with some prodding from Kurt, which helped speed up their progress through the city.

"I have to warn you," Peter wheezed, "You're going to have to do some things that you don't want to. Damage Control are going to find out about what's going on, if we're lucky."

Kurt wanted to quip back at him, but settled on business. "Will it help?"

"In the aftermath, yes," Peter said. "If we get there."

The creature had wrapped its tentacles around Ha'penny Bridge, while it tried to scoop up passers-by. Kurt was relieved that it hadn't grown any larger, but he was aware of the energy in the air changing. The teleportation spell was activating.

That was the least pressing concern. A car was suspended over the Liffey, held up with tentacles while a sharp-toothed mouth awaited feeding. "Somebody help," a man shouted from the car.

"Crap. This is what you were talking about, isn't it?" Kurt examined the situation. There was no way of getting the man out of the car telekinetically without further exposing him to the monster's teeth. "I'm going to have to break my one rule, aren't I?"

"Sorry," Peter muttered.

"Nevermind. No time to second guess myself." He concentrated on the man, on the space around him, on the movement and air flow, anything but the looming threat that awaited him, and clicked his fingers.

For most people, this would not do much. For a person like Kurt, experienced as he was with the mystical arts that he had earned the title Magic Man, a click of the fingers could change a small piece of the universe. He could tear down a house, or freeze a river, or burn a forest. He could summon a creature made from stone, or put a person to sleep, or build a stairway out of air. Or, though he had refrained from doing so for the longest time, he could teleport someone from one place to another.

The man vanished from the car just as teeth snapped through the engine. He landed in front of Kurt, saved from faceplanting by the magician. "Get out of here, okay?" Kurt said to him. "And don't speak of this to anyone."

The man nodded and ran. The crowds weren't far behind him as people emptied from the shops along the Quays by the river. The commotion was too much for the monster to pick up on. It was attempting to predict the easiest targets, while hundreds of people made minute decisions about which way to turn and how not to bump into each other, and where they would hide. Kurt could feel its frustration pouring from it.

Peter knew who would escape easily. The bigger picture unfolded in his mind while be tried to find Kurt's next best move. "We're running out of time," Peter told him. "If that spell activates, we're all dead. If Damage Control get here before the creature is killed, they're all dead. You need to hurry."

"What about the people?" Kurt asked.

"Distract it, restrain it, do something, and they'll be fine. Alive, at least." Pain was written all over his face, his features twisted and straining. "I'll give you a shout when you need a warning," Peter said to him. "Just let loose. I need to sit down."

Kurt didn't like to abandon Peter, but he had little choice. He clapped his hands together and summoned a few dozen chains from the walls along the Liffey. They pierced the monster's body and tentacles, burning at it, holding it in place, and thoroughly pissing it off. It glared at Kurt, so far the only person who had caused it pain. With its attention on him, the people were free to run.

There was no way he could hold back. Ice magic shot from his fingertips, freezing the water and the tentacles. The weight caused the creature to fall apart and regrow, while it struggled to get closer to him.

"They call me the Magic Man for a reason," he jeered. "It's time you understood the extent of my abilities, demon."

Kurt's eyes glowed, a dramatic and wasteful demonstration of power that accompanied a shift in the weather. The sky darkened overhead, clouds gathering over the monster. They swirled in one spot, bursting with energy. People were beginning to slow down, enamoured by the sudden display of defiance against the monster that threatened to consume them.

"Leave," Kurt roared, and they needed his words. There was a rumbling of thunder in the clouds. "Your extra eye allows you to see the future. So look, and witness your own suffering."

Stormbearing was an ancient magic. It could destroy a city if left unchecked, but it was less devastating than an angel's smiting. People could survive it, for a start. The true beauty of it, Kurt's primary reason for unleashing the power upon the city, was the random nature of lightning. There was no defence against the lightning without completely giving into protection over consumption.

"I have a theory, you know. You need to eat to feed this spell in the water. If I starve you, you'll be stuck here, or the spell will destroy you. Either way, London survives and you don't mutate any further. You'll be stuck in this battle until the cavalry arrives, and this turns into a full-scale assault."

The beast roared, tearing chains out of itself as a matter of pride. The freedom it was granted was enough to threaten

Kurt. Even with lightning raging down on it, tearing away at it, it came closer.

Fireballs from his palms did little to hold it back. Ice did nothing to slow it down. Stone jaws from the ground held back stray tentacles and walls of light severed others, but still the monster came closer. Kurt was running out of time and out of spells, and soon the creature would focus all of its attention in the present and the future on defeating him. It would be unstoppable, unbeatable, if it could put an end to the Magic Man who defied it.

He didn't think it knew anything about the potential attack from Kerubiel, or the notion of Damage Control and their arsenal of magical weapons that they would no doubt be bringing to try stop *him*. He hoped the display of magic would be enough would be enough to demonstrate that there was a specific reason he was there. They needed to come prepared, and he needed to not die.

"Kurt, behind you," Peter shouted.

The road lifted up in a domed shield behind Kurt just as a tentacle came within smashing distance. Kurt swore. "Thanks Peter. Now get to safety."

The fortune teller shook his head. "You need my help. You need to stop it, now." He fought his own instincts, and added, "I know how you can kill it."

Kurt joined the fortune teller, placing up a protective barrier between them and the beast. It was trying its best to break through. "Tell me. Quickly, precisely."

"The monster is just a shell. It has souls inside it. You have to separate them from the body." He sighed heavily. "I just don't know how you can do that."

"Simple," Kurt told him, "My best friends are a necromancer and a Reaper. I know exactly what to do."

A tentacle, mid-swing, exploded as it neared Kurt. Another froze. A third turned to stone. Determination and Peter's courage, combined with the splintering of Kurt's sanity by the Mind's Eye, gave him a shield that the monster couldn't break through.

Kurt opened his bag of formerly protective spells. Breaking spells open and turning them into something new was a hobby of Kurt's. He threw them one after the other at the creature. As they exploded, some ripped away pieces of watery flesh, while others functioned as if the opposite of shielding spells. Transparent barriers and mystical limbs sprouted out of thin air, blocking the monsters path in some directions, tugging at it from others, severing tentacles and keeping it trapped.

While it struggled against the spells, Kurt soared into the air on a gust of wind, the storm raging overhead. He reached out for the spells in the water, dragging the energy out of them. Knowing their proper usage, and so empowered as he was he began to redirect it. The storm funnelled downwards against the creature, sucking up the river around it, lightning tearing into the monster's flesh.

It screamed, and for the first time Kurt could feel the humanity trapped inside. "I'm sorry," he whispered.

Gary, in his role as a Reaper, had warned Kurt against the use of soul magic. Part of this had to do with his principal job, to collect and protect the souls of all living beings. Aside from that, though, he presented the use of soul magic as being detrimental to Kurt's own soul. It would expose him in ways he had never experienced. He could risk more than he could ever imagine by tapping into the magic of necromancy and soul manipulation.

That didn't stop Arnold teaching Kurt how to work the spells, should the need ever arise. There was an art to it, something that could be taught to only the most dedicated students. When it came to the study of magic, Kurt was the greatest student there had ever been. An extended life had helped, but the determination to learn more was a simple fact of his existence.

His hands burned as he charged the spell. Purple light seared the air and scorched the monster's chest. The lizard screamed as a hole grew, and for the first time a woman could be seen inside the beast.

Edward's words, as written in his letter, rang through Kurt's mind. "The first victim," he gasped. "The one who started it all. Gods, she's just trapped in there." He turned to look down at the ground. "Peter, are you seeing this?"

The psychic stared at the woman in awe. Kurt couldn't hear his response over the wind, but he imagined it to be some declaration about Jesus Christ.

"I have to get her out of there," he said to himself, and pulled as much magic as he could back from his active spells towards himself. "Here goes nothing."

With a second blast of light, this one white and shining, breaking up the clouds and creating a stillness in the water, the woman was forced away from the monster. It screamed, trying to lash out at him while green light poured from the gaping hole where its heart should have been. The woman rose into the air, a dozen souls or more wailing alongside her.

"Go," Kurt told her. The Mind's Eye was fully open now, and he watched her smile back at him. She mouthed a thank you, her eyes glazed over and her whole form weakening. One by one the souls of the dead, consumed by the lizard mouth over the past few nights, disappeared. The woman was last. She waved a goodbye to Peter and to Kurt, and slipped away to the Great Beyond.

Without her, the monster began to lose its physical form. The foresight it had used to fight Kurt so proficiently disappeared, and the tentacles became inactive. They melted into harmless puddles as they crashed against the roads on either side of the river.

The lizard roared as it disappeared, pouring into the river bit by bit until the scream died.

Silence fell over Dublin, and the Magic Man descended from the sky.

Chapter Thirteen: See No Evil

There was no such thing as a graceful landing when free-falling from forty feet up. Kurt Crane, in all his efforts to save the city, to stop the massacre at the Liffey, to prevent global catastrophe, had no more energy left to save himself. He fell onto an abandoned car on the North side of the river, crumpling the roof.

Peter was at his side in moments. "You know, I think this is the same car that hit you," he said with a weak laugh. "Are you alright, Kurt?"

"I think I broke a couple of ribs," the detective responded. "I'll heal. I always do. At least I finally got my revenge on the guy who ran me over." He lay there, still, while sirens filled the air. He didn't need Peter to tell him that help was coming. "What's the damage to the city like?" he asked, unable to make himself move.

Peter surveyed the scene from where he stood. "The walls along the river are in bits. A good few people are in the water, now. I think most of them are injured. The thing must have grabbed them. God, I can't believe someone was inside that the whole time. What was she doing in there?"

The question had been playing on Kurt since he'd seen her. "I think she was a battery. And the reason that it could predict my every move. Her body had been broken down by the time I got to her. She was just a soul wrapped up in magic. Every time that thing ate, another soul joined her. Someone was collecting."

"Seems a pretty extreme way of going about that," Peter muttered. "So, it's over? No more monster in the river?"

Kurt smiled. "Just the ones that belong there. I think an evicted troll is going to appreciate getting his home back." He sat upright as the sirens came closer and looked at the carnage behind him. People had been caught in the battle, even after they'd tried to leave. They'd been hit by stray tentacles and broken bricks. A couple had been hit by the tail ends of spells, though they would heal up alright. "We need to get out of here before someone starts asking me questions about how I stopped that thing."

He climbed uneasily from the car, and Peter grabbed him. He wrapped one of Kurt's arms over his shoulders, taking some of his weight while they hobbled away.

They couldn't return to the hotel, not yet. There would be too much suspicion, and Kurt had a feeling they wouldn't be welcome if someone was looking for him. The Dagda Inn only had so much patience. Peter led them back up Liffey Street, away from the water and the injured people, across the Luas line before the emergency services blocked the way completely.

Kurt stopped. "I need to sit down," he pleaded. "It's all hitting me now. The magic use, the pain, the exhaustion. I really need to stop."

Peter refused to let him go. "Not here. Someone's coming." He gasped. "I can still see the future. A bit. It's not as clear as before, but... Kurt, I didn't lose it all." He looked around the immediate vicinity, and steered Kurt just inside the doors of a supermarket. "This should be fine."

Kurt sank to the ground as the sky erupted. Dozens of lights descended in a flash on the city. People were appearing out of nowhere, and they weren't being subtle about it.

"Damage Control," Kurt explained. "They're here for the clean up. Fix the city, create a story, explain the losses. Put everything back as neatly as possible." He tensed up as a woman in a suit passed the door in front of them. Kurt remembered her from the Underground in London. At least he knew which branch was on the scene.

"What do we do?" Peter asked him.

"We sit tight. There's a small perception filter up around us at the moment. If she doesn't hang around, we'll be okay. I can hold it for a little while."

He closed his eyes against the strain. She was alone, a lost girl in a new city who didn't know what she was looking for, he thought. And she wouldn't move.

"I don't get it, we saved the day. I mean, you did most of the work, but we didn't do anything wrong."

Kurt grinned at Peter's naivety. "Some would argue that flying over the city while controlling the weather is wrong. I risked the total exposure of the magical community, today. Saved a lot of lives, sure, but potentially put a lot more at risk. You think the bad guys would hold back knowing they can't do any worse for secrecy than I did?"

Everything anyone did with magic had to be as close to a secret as possible. Even the people trying to cause harm did so in the quietest way possible until there was no way to stop them. The moment everyone knew about magic was the moment the plans and hard work would all fall apart. A demon summoner in a office would be discovered in an instant if people knew what to look for. A vampire who chose not to risk exposure to sunlight would be outed in an instant.

No one could do worse in the short term than expose themselves and others.

"This should have been over a few days ago. Now they'll resort to breaking taboo to keep mum about magic." He thought back to his chase through London. "You've seen *Men in Black*, I'm assuming. That, on a bigger scale."

"Memory wiping? Really?"

"Really." The woman finally moved on, and Kurt relaxed. "They'll start by getting the full story from people.

That's a lot of interviews. More will be on their way. They'll have the city on lockdown, soon, and no one will even notice."

Peter couldn't contain his anxiety. "Okay, wait here a second." He ran into the supermarket, leaving Kurt on lookout for more suited and booted members of Damage Control. Peter thrust a bottle of water, a bag of peanuts and a chocolate bar into his hands when he returned. "Water, salt, sugar. You're going to need them, right?"

"What are you seeing?"

Peter shook his head. "Just anxiety, really."

Kurt put a hand on his shoulder. "It's never just anxiety. Not when you can see the future." He told Peter about Edward's letter, and the way precognitive abilities could mess with mental health issues. He hoped he wasn't scaring the fortune teller. "So tell me, while I eat and drink and try not to throw up, what's plaguing your mind?"

Peter took a deep breath, an attempt to gather his thoughts and settle his mind. "Damage Control. They're going to be looking for you specifically in about ten minutes. Someone is going to describe what they saw, and they've put you right in the middle of their narrative. You're going to be hunted, Kurt."

Kurt struggled to his feet. "Okay, hotel management be damned, that's the best place for me." He leaned on Peter as they left the shelter of the building. "When we get there, you need to leave. You need to get somewhere safe, far away from me."

"I know," Peter said, winking. "Future vision, remember. If I stay, the hotel will be less lenient. They don't know me. But… someone owes you a favour?"

Kurt laughed, which hurt, but the relief and the capacity to let loose was worth it. "Someone always owes me a favour. It's what happens when you've been alive for as long as I have."

Henry Street was full of people, and it took some time to get through the crowds. Everyone was waiting for something, some sign that they could go home, or a check up from the emergency services for one injury or another. Kurt would have loved to help them, if he didn't feel like one more spell was going to break him completely. He could barely hold back the pain from his broken bones any longer. He needed Peter to push a path for them, or find the best route with the dregs of his ability.

O'Connell Street wasn't much better, but people were at least spread out a little bit further. Peter could find the hotel himself, while Kurt grimaced against the stabbing in his chest.

"The magic is part of you, now," he said hoarsely. "A slow infection drawing out something buried inside."

"Infection? My body is a temple, I'll have you know," Peter retorted.

The receptionist wasn't happy to see them, but he allowed Peter to bring Kurt upstairs. "No more jumping through windows," he warned them as they left the lobby.

"It was the rivers," Kurt explained. "The first victim of the time magic was in the Liffey. The magic affected you and Edward, too. One on each side of the teleportation spell." He sank into the armchair. "Sometimes, time magic has an agenda of its own, like a person in its own right." His head began to ache. "And sometimes, someone else is pulling the strings to try keep the world afloat."

Peter sat at the end of the bed. "Do you feel like explaining that one?"

Kurt shook his head. "It's a long story. The next time I'm in Dublin and there isn't a monster to slay, we'll grab a drink. I've heard of this great bar run by fairies with a taste for Death Metal."

"Is this a goodbye, Kurt?"

The magician made an effort to look at Peter when be addressed him. "Not if I can help it. I'll be wanting to check in on you."

Peter nodded, slowly. There was a grimace on his face. "I have one more warning for you," he said. "Not many details. I can't see too clearly, at the moment. But danger is coming for you, Kurt." He choked on his words, but he forced himself to continue. "You're going to die."

He left Kurt after that. The Magic Man didn't have a response. He always died. That was the arrangement. If his sacrifice could keep another person safe, it was worth it, every time.

He wondered how many times he had told himself that, and how many times it had felt like a lie.

"Just one more piece of business," he whispered, sitting up in the chair. He looked directly in to the mirror again. "I'm done," he said clearly. "I want you to take it back, now."

A hand print appeared on the mirror, as if on the other side. It pushes against the glass, slender fingers reaching out for him. There was a distinct feel of reality bending magic in the air. The hotel wouldn't be too pleased, Kurt thought.

The hand was cold to the touch when it planted its index finger on Kurt's forehead. The Mind's Eye was drawn away from him, and the world was suddenly much plainer. At the same time, he could think more clearly, and his sense of smell was returning to him, carrying the scent of Peter's breath and broken magic up Kurt's nose. There was a burning of ozone where the lightning had rippled around him in the storm.

The hand sank back into the mirror. No words were exchanged. Nothing could be said.

"See you in another life, Madame Madness," he said to the mirror, though he knew she was gone. He tried not to think about how soon that might be, with Peter's warning ringing through his head.

And then, with no more energy left but what he'd gotten from the snacks at the supermarket, he fell asleep.

The case, as far as psychics and monsters were concerned, was finally closed.

Paul Carroll

Epilogue

For Kurt Crane, the Magic Man, the detective, one of the most wanted men on the planet, nothing really ends. Between jobs, in the old days, there was trouble. Between troubles were problems, and between the problems, issues. Everything else was time spent waiting.

He had waited for nearly thirty years, now, to find himself back in his old habits. He had been back in London barely a day when he grew restless. His ribs were still tender, but healing magic had done him a great deal of good. It had meant calling in a favour, but it had been worth it to reduce the risk of a lung puncture.

Still tired and a little bit sore all over, he was lying on his bed. There was only one thing he could think about doing, and one thing he didn't want to do. One option meant being a good friend, the other meant being a mature adult. He knew which one was preferable, and which could wait until the other was done.

So he called Arnold.

"I can't believe you," Arnold said immediately.

"Hello to you, too, Arnold. I suppose you've heard about what happened."

There was some swearing down the other end of the line, which was finally punctuated with, "You should have told us."

"You need *my* help, remember. I couldn't ask for you to come all the way here. Or to Dublin." He smiled to himself. It felt good to talk to someone closer to his age who knew what the work was all about. "Anyway, I'm not dead, and I saved the world, so it's no big deal."

The line muffled on Arnold's side. "Gary says you're an idiot, but he's glad you're okay. He also wants to talk to you, but I said no." The pair argued some more on the other end of the line. "Dublin is fine, he says. Memories wiped, all cleaned up. Damage Control lost you. They wanted to break into the Dagda Inn to try find you, but they weren't allowed."

"There are rules for a reason," Kurt joked.

"Look, it's a bit worse than that, though. Great that the city was saved and all, but they did a post-mortem on that guy you sent in. Edward Armstrong? Death by Hellfire, Kurt." This wasn't surprising news, and Arnold seemed puzzled. "Okay, maybe Hellfire isn't a big deal to you anymore, so how about I clarify. They have a specialist in the field. It wasn't just any old demon. It was a Greater Demon's power that charged what spell. Whatever mess you've got yourself involved in, it just got a little bit messier."

Kurt laughed out loud, which seemed to annoy Arnold more than anything. "I'll be fine, Arn. I'm ready to join you. You still need my help?"

The mood changed. There was a childlike joy to Arnold's voice when he responded. "Oh, like you wouldn't believe, Kurt. You know that old duster you used to wear? The one with all the warding spells and protection charms?"

Kurt knew it well. It had been hanging up in his office for nearly thirty years slowly smelling more and more like stale cigar smoke. It was the ultimate protection anyone hunting demons could ask for.

"What about it?"

"Grab it, and head to the old burial ground. You know the spot?"

It was where they had 'buried' Kurt in the 1950s. His body never quite made it into the grave, but it was a fixed location. "I know it," Kurt said. "What will I do when I get there?"

"Walk on your grave, Kurt. I'll handle the rest." He seemed giddy down the other end of the phone. "We'll see you soon, buddy. We missed you."

"You too, Arnold."

The lines disconnected, and Kurt packed a bag. He needed to make one quick stop at the office to grab his duster jacket, dreading the idea of wearing it during the American summer. He looked back at the envelopes left unopened on his bookshelf. They could wait.

The job was over, but the work still awaited. It was time to save the world. Again

Paul Carroll

Acknowledgements

This book started as an idea in college about a man who constantly came back from the dead, which has felt like an extended metaphor for my professional and personal life. With that in mind, I need to start by thanking the friends who stuck with me during some of the most difficult parts of my life over the last year.

Gareth Luby has been a greater friend than I deserve, and helped me escape both the horror of unemployment and a creative block that lasted much longer than I would have liked. Gary Moloney has been a valuable writing partner, whose friendship and support has enabled me to rethink my writing processes and approaches to stories. Helen Carroll and Kat Dodd have been true friends, and provide both a source of encouragement and a place for me to figure things out.

As well as Helen and Kat, I need to thank the rest of Cupán Fae: Tommy, Catherine, Roisin, Sorcha, Yvonne, Quinn, Leyla, Mark, Axel, Eoghan, Ryan, Caitriona, Ellen, and Colm.

A special thanks goes out to Ian Mac An Ghaill, the fastest reader I know and a valuable editing assistant. Ian makes my books better.

Thanks to my family, who have been patient with me while I worked on this book, and who provide occasional necessities like tea and homemade cake.

Thanks to the friends who continually provide support and express an interest in my writing.

And finally, thank you to everyone who has picked up this or another book from me over the years. It means the world to me that I get to share my stories with people.

About the Author

Paul Carroll is a writer and comic creator from Dublin.

His work primarily focuses on the extraordinary, be that through magic, science or just downright chaotic. He is a founding member of both Limit Break Comics and Cupán Fae, Dublin-based creative groups. His obsessions include tea, foxes and spreadsheets.

For free stories, news and updates, visit
paulcarrollwriter.com

Printed in Poland
by Amazon Fulfillment
Poland Sp. z o.o., Wrocław

62799260R00094